Fair
Game

A Salt Mine Novel

Joseph Browning   Suzi Yee

Text Copyright © 2021 by Joseph Browning and Suzi Yee

Published by Expeditious Retreat Press
Cover by J Caleb Design
Edited by Elizabeth VanZwoll

For information regarding Joseph Browning and Suzi Yee:

Subscribe to their mailing list at their website: https://www.joseph-browning.com

To follow them on Twitter: https://twitter.com/Joseph_Browning

To follow Joseph on Facebook: https://www.facebook.com/joseph.browning.52

To follow Suzi on Facebook: https://www.facebook.com/SuziYeeAuthor/

To follow them on MeWe: https://mewe.com/i/josephbrowning

By Joseph Browning and Suzi Yee

THE SALT MINE NOVELS

Money Hungry	Hen Pecked	Dark Matter
Feeding Frenzy	Brain Drain	Silent Night
Ground Rules	Bone Dry	Deep Sleep
Mirror Mirror	Vicious Circle	Home Grown
Bottom Line	High Horse	Better Half
Whip Smart	Fair Game	Mortal Coil
Rest Assured	Double Dutch	

Chapter One

Dr. Elijah Jenkin looked down at his phone and grumbled when he saw the time. This was his sixth year working the Institute of Tradition's booth at the Minnesota State Fair—the third in charge—and he'd honed the setup of the twenty-by-twenty endcap to an art. First, the signage was hung and the freestanding structures were assembled. Then, the folding tables were positioned and dressed with their signature purple tablecloths, laboriously embroidered in different cultural motifs using a wide array of needlecraft. Last, the merchandize was racked: dozens of issues of the Institute's magazine, *The Way Things Were.*

With his planning and the help of his four-person team, it should have done and dusted by now except the pallet of periodicals had yet to be delivered to the booth and each phone call he'd made was met with the same answer: it will be there before the end of the day. His crew was getting restless with nothing to do. *Many hands make light work but idle hands are the devil's tools*, he aphorized to himself. The only saving grace was that the wifi was working and not at a snail's pace.

The cavernous building had reached peak warmth as it soaked in the August sun all day. Coupled with the frenetic energy of a hall full of vendors and machinery, it was downright steamy. It had air-conditioning, but that wouldn't be turned on until later this evening, after all the in-and-out traffic was done; the fair didn't pay to cool the outside.

This wasn't where Jenkin imagined himself when he'd graduated from the University of Minnesota with an Anthropology doctorate six years ago. He'd assumed he would be teaching at some university while aggressively applying for grant money to conduct more field research to enhance his already impressive publishing CV. The thought of taking a job in the private sector never even occurred to him, especially after all the digs he'd received about how unemployable his degree was while he was in school.

At his mother's insistence, he'd attended a local job fair and that's when the Institute of Tradition pinged on his radar. It was an international organization dedicated to documenting and preserving the local traditions and stories of peoples and places, with a branch on every continent—excluding Antarctica, of course. The head office for North America was in Detroit, but the printing branch was in Minneapolis.

Every quarter, the branch produced an issue of *The Way Things Were* and they were looking for editorial staff. Jenkin had been skeptical at first. He knew of the publication's reputation and he wasn't sure if it would be a good fit. For more than seventy years, it had straddled its two main demographics—the scientific and the broader-minded—by packing each issue with histories, legends, and beliefs alongside a hefty dose of the occult and other matters which could only be termed as *alternative.*

He'd broken down and applied for the position when the grace period on his student loans was dwindling and there were no bites on the other lines he had cast in the water. He immediately signed on when he saw the pay and benefits package and that grew into a new career that eventually led to his fourteenth-story private office with a lovely view overlooking the city—a far cry from his current environs.

Jenkin wiped the sweat from his brow and considered making yet another call. The venue would shut the freight doors for deliveries in a little bit, but the vendors didn't have to have everything ready until an hour before the doors officially opened to the public tomorrow. He didn't relish cutting it that close, but he would if he must. Just as he was about to press dial, he heard the beep of moving machinery: a loaded forklift coming in hot.

"Watch out for the tables!" Jenkin scolded the driver. The tablecloths would be laundered after the fair was over, but he'd be damned if they got grease stains or damage from a careless operator before the fair even started.

The driver scowled at him—he knew what he was doing

and he wasn't anywhere *close* to the tables. To prove his point, he threaded the opening into the endcap and dropped the pallet smack dab in the middle, ignoring Jenkin's gestures to place it to the side.

"Sorry pal, gotta keep the aisles clear," he hollered over the blaring reverse alarm and drove away with a smirk on his face. *Question my forking, will yah?*

The crew descended on the pallet with box cutters and keys, tearing away at the shell of plastic wrap before systematically unpacking the boxes within. As each box was removed, Jenkin checked its contents against the bill of lading and the foursome grouped them by issue number and promotional material.

Space was limited in the booth. In order to maximize browsing for customers and ensure that restocks were always on hand, the boxes were stored under the tables, tucked behind the tablecloths until it was time to pack up at the end of the fair. Jenkin had a diagram of where each box should be placed based on issue number for restocking and marked each slot with a post-it note. While the muscle was matching and stacking, the others started filling the sales racks. The Institute of Tradition booth was once again a hive of activity, filled with purpose.

Jenkin exited the endcap and walked around, examining it from the perspective of fairgoers. "Mee, can you reverse the order on the table rack? I still want them in chronological order, but if we flip them, it puts the most-recent issue at eye level."

"Got it, Elijah," she replied. The young Asian woman

immediately reversed her hands, taking magazines off the rack and rearranging them before setting them back. She was the kind of person that didn't have to be told the same thing twice.

"Josh, only put out three or four of each promotional item at a time. We'll run out otherwise," Jenkin suggested. The curly-haired man with small circular glasses nodded as he returned the excess tchotchkes back to their respective boxes. He boggled at why someone would grab a handful of pens or keychains just because they were there and free, but he bowed to Jenkin's expertise.

In no time, the booth looked right and the empty pallet and trash from setup was placed in the aisle for pick up. "Looks good," Jenkin praised them. "Let's get everything covered and get some Juicy Lucys." The pack of hungry young twenty-somethings salivated at the thought of burgers with the cheese stuffed in the middle of the patty. There were always a few food vendors that set up early—someone had to feed the people working the fair before the public descended on the grounds.

"And cold beers?" Kevin Smoll cheekily suggested. "Moving all those boxes worked up a thirst."

"Are you all twenty-one?" Jenkin asked cautiously.

They all looked to Mee Vang, universally known to be the youngest of the group. She was barely out of school and was recently hired as a web developer. The petite woman defiantly pursed her lips and met their collective gaze with her pert upturned nose. "I'll have you know, I've been twenty-one for a whole month."

Jenkin shrugged. "Then Juicy Lucys and cold beers all around," he announced. "Then we have to meet the others in front of the Haunted Mansion."

There was a collective groan as they went outside despite the welcomed fresh air and a stunning setting sun that splashed a kaleidoscope of colors on the stark concrete and green agricultural building behind them. "I know some of you find it corny," Jenkin interjected, "but it comes with the territory."

"What exactly are we doing?" Vang asked. It was her first fair as an Institute employee and she hadn't paid much attention to the details after she'd read free passes with a per diem for food and vendor parking.

"Nothing hard—walk around the fairgrounds, chant some stuff, and toss some flour in the air periodically," Smoll replied nonchalantly. "At least it's not raining."

"And you do this every year?" Vang said incredulously. "Why?"

Josh Henderson, who worked in accounting, fielded her question. "Because some old biddy or superstitious coot tied their bequeathment to performing that specific task. You'd be surprised how much of our funding comes with such stipulations. Some want prayers said over graves at certain times, others want saucers of milk left out for the wee folk. It really varies."

"Couldn't you just say you did it?" she ventured, but she

8

immediately knew it was the wrong thing to say by the utter and immediate silence of her compatriots.

"We honor the wishes of all our benefactors, even the kooky ones," Jenkin replied diplomatically.

"Plus, the last thing we need is an auditor breathing down our necks," Henderson added. The seasoned employees all voiced their agreement, and Vang understood the implication even if she was fuzzy on the particulars. Audit was a dirty word in her house growing up. As much as her parents hated paying taxes, the idea of being audited was even worse.

"It's really not that bad," the fourth member of the team chimed in. The willowy blonde with the pixie haircut spoke from experience; Michelle Giles had been in charge of their social media presence for three years and the worst she'd been asked to do was burn some fat rolls of sage and hang particular crystals in specific geometric orientations to protect against evil spirits. "You generally get to pick which ones you do. Better to suck it up, do it right, and make sure there's plenty of money to keep the operation going."

Vang bobbed her head side to side. "Doesn't sound all that different from the random stuff my grandparents have us do for good luck." Despite her easygoing response, Jenkin suspected she had her reservations when he caught her unconsciously straightened the crucifix hanging around her neck while they waited for food.

The conversation moved to more banal topics as they ate.

The sun had set fully by the time they were finished and they strolled leisurely with sated bellies. They were halfway to their destination when the midway tested the lights. A flood of neon cascaded down the street and the music from the various rides suddenly started mid-song. Bathed in every color of the rainbow, the sparse crowd clapped and cheered at the herald of yet another Minnesota State Fair. Tomorrow night, it would be packed with visitors, but tonight, it was just theirs: the people that made the fair a magical place.

The lights brought Jenkin's crew to a halt. "Makes you feel like a kid again," Smoll said wistfully.

Giles nodded. "When the footlongs were as long as your arm."

"And they still gave out goldfish as prizes, " Henderson added.

Jenkin smiled. He remembered what it was like in one's early twenties: just old enough to feel the first pangs of nostalgia. Not a kid anymore, but not quite a full-grown adult either. "We'll see how fond you are after you smell like fry oil for two weeks," he teased them and broke their revelry. "We'd better get moving. Richard is a stickler about being on time."

Jenkin may have been the leader of the booth, but Richard Orhan was in charge of executing tonight's bequeathment request correctly, and no one wanted to get on his bad side. To call him imposing was an understatement.

Even though he was thin, as though every bit of excess

weight had gone straight into his height, his towering six-foot-seven frame made everyone feel smaller than they were. His fastidiously trimmed Van Dyke was just starting to show a little gray, and it wasn't hard to imagine him sinisterly twirling the ends with his fingertips. His personality and wit did little to soften his appearance. He was the kind of person who signed office birthday cards "regards" and always went by his full name, as anyone who tried to call him "Rich" had learned.

Jenkin's evocation of the man had its intended effect and they picked up the pace, coming within sight of the Haunted Mansion in no time. It was a two-story dark mauve building trimmed in black with a pair of massive Corinthian columns holding up the porch. Originally a square block of four separate apartments, the neo-classical building had been renovated ages ago into a traditional house of horrors. It was campy and dated in comparison to modern haunted houses, more akin to Scooby Doo spooky, but it was part and parcel of the fairgrounds. People went to it year after year, the same way some families always rode It's a Small World whenever they went to Disney, regardless how old they were or how many times they had already been.

There was a small group milling outside the building and Jenkin recognized them as colleagues. Most were dressed in normal street clothing, but a few—including Orhan—were wearing ceremonial robes.

"Elijah, you made it," Orhan called out, waving one of his

massive hands at him. "Any trouble at the booth?"

"Nothing that didn't work itself out," Jenkin responded truthfully. "The booth is ready for tomorrow."

"Good. I know you know the drill, but for the rest of you…" the giant's baritone rumbled as he handed each of Jenkin's crew a small pamphlet from the hemp bag slung around his torso. "Instructions for tonight," he explained in brief.

Vang accepted the well-worn saddle-stitched pamphlet from the stark man. Her entire hand would easily fit in the confines of just his palm. She turned on the flashlight app on her phone so she could read it in the dark.

As Jenkin drifted away to greet the others, Giles slid beside Vang and gave her the scoop, now that they were no longer amongst upper management. "It's not unlike going to mass— just mumble along and copy what the rest do and you'll be fine," she muttered under her breath.

"How did you know I was Catholic?" Vang whispered.

"Takes one to know one," Giles answered playfully and pulled out her own crucifix. She gave Vang a wink before tucking it back under her shirt. "Just stick with me and do what I do. And don't stand downwind—you'll get covered in flour."

Vang smiled. "I can do that."

With the addition of five more, Orhan had enough participants to proceed, but he did a quick headcount—literally at his height—to be sure.

He projected his voice above the chatter. "All right ladies and gentlemen, let's get started. Tonight we will be performing the same ritual at three different locations to placate the spirits, all of which must be completed before the stroke of midnight." Vang's body tensed at the word *ritual*. It smacked of unsavory things she'd been warned about numerous times throughout her brief life—devil worship, pagans, and witches to name a few.

"What does he mean by 'ritual'?" she asked Giles as everyone else collected their things.

"Nothing nearly as deviant as you're imagining," she answered.

"What are you two whispering about?" Henderson inserted himself into the conversation as the group fell into step behind Orhan.

"Just walking Mee through the ropes of her first 'ritual,'" Giles explained with air quotes.

Henderson rolled his eyes. "Everything's a ritual to him. He's super into all this. I wouldn't be surprised if he had pagan goat pants in the back of his closet."

"It's always the quiet ones," Giles obliquely agreed.

Vang giggled and relaxed a little. She generally worked in a bubble and this was her first foray at making work friends since she'd started at the Institute.

The walk was brief—just around the corner, past the State Fair Dairy Building, and onto Bazaar Road. Everyone gathered into a circle on the concrete parking lot to the south and Vang stayed close to Giles and Henderson, who took pains to position themselves upwind.

Orhan nodded to the guy with a bodhrán, and the drummer produced a simple beat, a rich *thunk* that only came from thick animal hide. Orhan started chanting and the others quickly joined him. Vang followed along in the pamphlet and found Giles was right. Except for the content, it wasn't all that different than saying The Lord's Prayer during mass. There was even a section of call and response where Orhan said some bits in Latin and the rest repeated a chorus. *Be edified.*

The Celtic drum beat double time as Orhan pulled a black sack from his bag and walked around the circle, allowing each of them to take a handful of rye flour. When he returned to his position in the circle, he took a handful himself and the drummer gave the bodhrán a final powerful thwack, signaling everyone to throw the flour into the circle.

It landed in uneven patches in front of each person as the last beat of the drum hung in the air. As the taut skin of the bodhrán slowly ceased vibrating, the grains started shifting across the concrete on their own. A string of gasps sounded as people registered the movement. It started out slow, but quickly picked up speed until the flour sinuously formed a single word: HELP.

Chapter Two

Detroit, Michigan, USA
27th of August, 6:46 a.m. (GMT-4)

David Emrys Wilson—codename Fulcrum—felt a slight pawing on his arm. He rolled over and tried to ignore it but it only grew more insistent. When he finally lay back and opened his eyes, he was met by the silky black cat that had become his roommate of a sort.

"Good morning, Mau," he garbled through a yawn. Her intense green eyes bore into him. The cat of legend prided herself on her ability to pretend to be a normal cat and answered with a simple meow, but telepathically, she sent two words: *You're late.* They felt like a scathing condemnation.

That can't be right? Wilson thought as he groggily turned his head to the side. It took a moment for him to register the time on the clock, but when he did, he cursed. He remembered waking at the rumble of the USPS fleet leaving the distribution center and pulling the blanket over his head, but he didn't recall dozing off again. He immediately kicked off the sheets and jumped out of bed.

"Why didn't you wake me sooner?" he asked her on his

way to the bathroom. There was no time for calisthenics this morning.

Because the fish from the metal circle wasn't late until now, she answered through the door. *Are you sick? Do you need a swnw?*

"What's a swnw?"

A healer, she replied simply. Sometimes she forgot he didn't know the true name of things.

"I'm fine. I just overslept. Why don't you wait in the kitchen? I'll only be a few minutes," he reassured her. It was his way of shooing her away so he could use the restroom in peace. It was hard enough trying to urinate with someone talking to you through the door, never mind telepathically.

He rushed through an abbreviated morning routine before grabbing a shirt, tie, and suit from the closet. He dressed in haste and wondered why he didn't smell coffee; his machine should have automatically made him a double at 6:45.

When he entered the kitchen, Mau was waiting by her bowl, flicking her tail impatiently. He bypassed the espresso machine and went straight to the pantry for a can of albacore. The feline watched with renewed interest as he opened the can and fluffed up the individual flakes with a fork. He poured the oil over the top before setting the silver dish on the floor. "Bon appetite." She pounced on the food and started the customary growling noises she made when she ate. He knew he was mostly forgiven when she let him pet her.

He rinsed out the tin and washed his hands at the sink

before investigating the matter of the absent coffee. Propped up against the unit was the business card   of Dr. Sylvia Kamiński, the same one Leader had given him months ago. He hadn't gotten around to making an appointment yet and surmised that Mau decided her late breakfast warranted another reminder. It wasn't the first time the card had magically appeared on his espresso machine.

He put the card in his suit pocket without saying a word. He hadn't brought up the fact that Leader had given it to him, and Mau hadn't mentioned that she was concerned about him, but here it was. Again. Mau didn't need words to make her opinion known.

Wilson began troubleshooting the blinking icon on the display screen, the definitive sign that all was not right. He started with the obvious: it was plugged in and had power. The clock was right, and the program to make his morning coffee was on. He knew he'd filled the water tank last night but checked it anyway. When he found it full, he moved to the hopper.

"Mau, have you been making yourself coffee when I'm at work?" he asked her as he opened the cupboard for more coffee beans to refill the empty chamber.

She sent him a telepathic guffaw, followed by *Only you drink the foul liquid.* He pressed a few buttons and grinned when the grinder started. Even his coffee was having a late start, but better that than never. He cobbled together breakfast on-the-go and added milk and sugar to his travel mug before heading in to work with his Korchmar Monroe attaché in hand.

Even though he was only ten minutes behind schedule, the roads were noticeably more congested. In the comfort of his British racing green 911, he endured the stop-and-go until he reached his exit. There was no through-traffic to Zug Island, and the only vehicles headed that direction were deliveries and employees of the two businesses that operated on the island.

To the guards at the entry gate, he was Davis Watson, Director of Acquisitions for Discretion Minerals—just another suit driving an expensive car who parked in an executive spot in the underground garage. It wasn't until he presented his titanium key in the elevator and descended into the earth that the ruse ended and he was once again fully himself.

"Good morning, Mr. Wilson," the bubbly voice of Angela Abrams greeted him as the elevator doors opened to the first floor of the Salt Mine. As usual, the attendant sat behind a barrier of ballistic glass but he noticed something different about her this morning.

"Good morning, Abrams. Trying something new with your hair?" he commented as he loaded his possessions into the metal slot for scanning and unholstered the Glock 26 resting under his jacket.

She gave him a coy look through her long lashes. "Trying strawberry blonde for the summer," she answered before turning her eyes to the screen to make sure nothing was wrong with him. Had it come from any of the other agents, she would have chalked it up to friendly small talk or flirtation, but Wilson did not readily engage in either.

"It suits you," he said stiffly and waited in awkward silence as the machines whirled. *That's more like it*, she thought as the monitors confirmed it was Wilson and his personal items were clean.

"Everything looks good. You can enter and pick up your things on the other side," she informed him over the tinny speaker. He strode through the now-open door and put his gun away before grabbing his briefcase. "Have a good day, Mr. Wilson."

"You as well, Abrams," he politely replied before going to the next set of elevators. He presented his eye and palm to the scanners and pressed level five.

He'd just wrapped up a case two days ago and had mission summation paperwork to complete as well as an expense report to file, which meant spending the morning in his subterranean office. He turned on the light and did a quick sweep, finding everything as he'd left it. He placed his things on the French polished walnut desk and pressed the desktop's power button. He hung his jacket on the hall tree and settled into the leather and walnut swivel chair that matched his Art Deco desk. While his computer booted, he skimmed the dailies over warm coffee and a cold breakfast. Culled from FBI and CIA briefings, the dailies were more of the same. As long as the world was plagued by so many conflicts, people like him would never be short of work.

As there was nothing else in his inbox, he dove straight into his report. It was a simple affair: a practitioner whose ambition outstripped their ability and was killed in the process. Once he'd ascertained it was a lone actor and not part of a larger plot, it was a matter of damage control: hunting down and banishing that which didn't belong in the mortal realm, removing magical items and text from the premises, padding the budget with any valuables, and cleansing tainted things with fire. Wilson had become used to cleaning up after dead magicians over the years. After so many, he was certain he could add "pre-morgue processing" and "crime scene simulation" to his resume.

He always wrote the case and expense report at the same time to make sure they were in alignment. He liked to stick to the facts: a series of short declarative sentences providing an accurate timeline to justify his actions and spent resources. It was part of the reason he sent regular updates to the Mine—he could access those later to refresh his memory on exactly when he knew what. It was a dry read, but made LaSalle's job easier when it came time for reimbursements. Once those were filed on the intranet, he putzed around his office until it was time for lunch.

In the past, working alone in his office was a perk, but after his time in Avalon, he found himself craving more social interaction despite the fact that he generally didn't like people.

If he wasn't completely engrossed in something, the walls started to hem in after a few hours. It was an odd conundrum to come to in one's forties and he'd taken to eating in the cafeteria to break up the isolation. Even though he ate alone, the near proximity to others was enough most days.

The Salt Mine never closed and neither did the cafeteria. There was always a cold case of sandwiches and wraps that changed in regular rotation along with drinks, fruit, and individually wrapped snacks for those eating off hours. Three times a day, hot meals were served buffet-style and the kitchen put out a decent spread.

The cafeteria was in a long rectangular room in the back of the first floor, accessible to everyone who worked in the Mine. It was pizza day, and Wilson loaded up his plate with a salad on the side and two pudding cups. Then he headed straight for a table where a lone blond man was arranging the components of his lunch to his satisfaction: ham and Emmental on a kaiser roll served with mustard, butter lettuce, and one slice of a beefsteak tomato.

Today, Wilson wasn't dining alone but with the Salt Mine's latest recruit: Hans Lundqvist, the middle of the three brothers he'd had cause to investigate recently. Hans had the rare ability to fuse magic and technology together, and the seed Wilson had planted a year ago bloomed when he'd finally tired of his brothers' shenanigans, especially after his eldest brother's wife Camille had left. He saw little reason to stay after she moved out; she'd been the only one that treated him with any real kindness.

"Hello, Hans," Wilson greeted him and took the opposite seat.

Hans's blue eyes looked up from his perfected sandwich and he made his "happy to see you" face as he responded in kind. "Hello, David."

It still felt weird being called by his given name, but not unpleasantly so. He was Fulcrum or Wilson to most of the people in the Mine and Crawling Shadow to Mau, but Hans always addressed him by his first name, now that he knew what it really was. He did this because Wilson was his friend and one addressed friends informally.

"I've never understood the American obsession with pizza," he commented on Wilson's tray. Others would have taken it as criticism, but Hans was just stating a fact.

Wilson shrugged. "When you grow up eating something, it seems normal."

Hans paused to process that and made a gesture that he found it acceptable before changing the subject. "Did you know forty percent of all mammal species are rodents?"

"I did not," Wilson answered his question, and Hans proceeded to tell him about the capybara, the largest rodent. Others might have questioned the wisdom in discussing rodents while eating, but it didn't bother either of them. They proceeded to exchange a series of factoids in a volley that had the verisimilitude of conversation.

At first, these shared meals were part of settling Hans into his new home, but Wilson had come to enjoy them. He found Hans's company less taxing than most because he didn't require the performative acts that others did when they socialized. Hans was direct and logical with little to no subtext in his interaction. If he didn't understand something, he'd ask for clarification. If he disagreed, he said so and why. To Hans, things were what they were and Wilson appreciated that.

"Aren't you going to finish your lunch?" Hans asked pointing to the two uneaten pudding cups on Wilson's tray.

"These aren't for me. They are for Chloe and Dot," he explained as they rose to bus their dishes. "I'm doing some reading in the library this afternoon."

The mention of the twins stirred something in Hans. "Chloe seems nice but I'm not sure Dot likes me."

"What makes you say that?" Wilson asked.

"Whenever I see her, she always looks mad."

Wilson bobbed his head side to side. "That doesn't necessarily mean she doesn't like you. Dot is often cross about something."

Hans considered it and deferred to Wilson's greater experience with the surlier of the conjoined sisters, but he had more evidence he felt compelled to present for completeness sake. "She doesn't always address me by my name."

Wilson raised an eyebrow. "What does she call you?"

"Weber's mini-me. Thing 2. Plan B," Hans listed the most recent ones he could remember.

Wilson fought the urge to smirk and got to the heart of the matter as they walked toward the elevators. "Does it bother you?"

Hans thought about it as they waited for the carriage. "Not particularly."

"Then I wouldn't worry about it," Wilson offered his two cents. "She doesn't like change and she'll probably come around in time. She respects indifference."

Hans nodded. He understood aversion to change. He was extremely relieved when he found an exact replica of his bedroom and workshop newly cut out of the salt on the sixth floor, and the kitchen always had his meals the way he wanted them when he wanted them. With the day-to-day affairs taken care of, he was free to concentrate on his work with Weber, who he liked quite a lot. Ever since Hans moved in, German had become the default language in the workshop when it was just the two inventors. Hans had always preferred German over English: he preferred languages with consistent spelling and grammar.

When the elevator arrived, Hans put his eye and palm to the scanners and pressed the button for the sixth floor. His access was limited to just the workshop and his private quarters, but Wilson took the opportunity to hitch a ride, saving the librarians the trouble of fetching him from the fifth floor.

They parted ways with succinct but friendly words and Wilson took the passage that led to the library. "I come bearing pudding," he announced when he saw the blonde heads staring down at their respective books at the circular desk.

Chloe looked up with a smile. "Sweet!"

Dot's eyes remained on the page as she asked, "What flavor?"

"Tapioca," he responded as he set the pudding cups down with two spoons.

"Right answer," Dot said as she closed her tome. "You here on a case or independent study?"

Chloe pulled off the top and licked it clean before grabbing a spoon. "Hi, Wilson. Thanks for the pudding. How are you doing today?" she said to remind her sister what manners sounded like.

Dot waved her hand dismissively. "He already knows all that."

"No case, just here to keep researching transmutation," he answered Dot's question.

Chloe nodded to a stack of books on the far table. "I picked out some reference materials that might help you conceptualize the processes better."

"I'm not advocating drug use, but it might help you understand the material better if you were high…" Dot drily cautioned him.

He chuckled. "Thanks, I'll keep that in mind." With the

offering accepted, he took a seat next to the collection of books. It seemed like a lot, but he didn't have to read each one cover to cover. He picked up the sheet of paper whose corner was secured by a tome and scanned the list of relevant passages scrawled in Chloe's flowery handwriting and started at the top.

With his augmentation training stalled, he'd decided to move to a different field of arcane study. During a recent mission, he'd sold himself as a maker and preserved the mushrooms of a fairy ring he was in the process of dismantling to appease a capricious hamadryad, who was even more lethal than she was beautiful. At the time, it had been taxing and he was simply trying not to get killed, but he discovered a deep satisfaction in the doing.

While Wilson was aces at security and summoning, he was a relative novice in other arcane disciplines because until Avalon, they'd made him as high as a kite. Lucky for him, he worked one floor above the most extensive stacks dedicated to the magical arts and run by the most knowledgeable librarians in the field.

When he'd first asked the twins for their help, they were almost as surprised as him. Dot especially found it hard to believe he was interested in such a creative field of magic. After she'd doled out the requisite amount of teasing, the pair had given him a reading list to refresh him on the fundamentals.

The most basic of transmutations bore striking resemblance to mere parlor tricks but there was more to it than that. It wasn't an illusion or projected charm, but an actual change in the target's nature. Its foundation was understanding what a thing was and then reimagining the manifestation of that thing.

The enchantment Wilson had done on the mushrooms was on the easy end of the spectrum. He'd seen the vibrant color before he'd uprooted each one and returning the color was a matter of restoring them to their originally experienced condition. It would have been a much harder task to change them to a different color and even more challenging to transmute the mushrooms into flowers.

Even though Wilson had done the scholastic work, he'd found the actual practice of transmutation quite a bit harder outside of the Magh Meall. The middle land was an enchanted place, a bridge between the world of man and fae. Magic flowed freely there and without karmic cost. In the mortal realm, changing the nature of things was not so easy. There was more inertial reality to overcome.

And that wasn't the only hurdle he had to overcome. Yet again, Wilson found himself going against type. Transmutation lent itself to practitioners creative in disposition: poets, painters, sculptors, philosophers, and those similarly touched with an artistic soul. Wilson was very good at imagining different scenarios and planning contingencies, but that was more methodical than creative. The closest he came to a generative endeavor was ward creation, and he approached that more like a puzzle.

This creativity meant that the writings of master transmuters could get a little out there. Some were a pure stream of consciousness while others tried more formal explanations, but it was like trying to read about how to dance—possible, but much less effective than being taught by someone who actually knew how. When he found something that resonated with him, he marked the source and made a few notes to jog his memory on the list Chloe had made for him.

He was in the middle of reading Jean-Baptiste-Louis-Théodore de Tschudi's *Etheric Sublimation* when he heard the phone at the circular desk ring. As the sociable one of the pair, Chloe answered and verbally promised to pass along the message. When she hung up the receiver, she called out to him. "Wilson, you're wanted on the fourth floor."

Chapter Three

Leader's mind was far away in time and space as she waited for LaSalle to hunt down Fulcrum. In her hands, she held a wooden disk with a hole in the middle. Thickest at the center, the unadorned cedar thinned toward the rim and its surface had been polished smooth by years of use.

Returning Alberia to her true form had been a joy in and of itself—she would have done it without the promise of a favor—but she was never one to waste an opportunity. What some considered mercenary, she called common sense. She hadn't survived this long by only relying on the kindness of others.

When the absconded Fomoir returned, Leader's standing with the fae as a whole rose, except with the houses that now constituted the newly reformed Dökkálfar. Her piety had been recently rewarded when a fae informant sent word that a plain cedar wand had recently exchanged hands in one of the seedier parts of the Magh Meall. Over the years, she'd uncovered many imitations, but she couldn't help but hope that this time it would be the real one: the one and only wand of Circe.

The ancient Greek witch was best remembered for her transmutation and potions, but she was also a master at the loom and produced fine enchanted cloth, and the gradual taper of her wand wasn't just for ease of grip; it also held a whorl to be used as a drop spindle. Leader held the whorl, but it wouldn't spin enchanted thread without its matching wand.

David LaSalle's crisp tenor streamed in through the small speaker on her desk, "Fulcrum has arrived."

The announcement pulled her back to the here and now. As the stark saline walls absorbed the resonance of her assistant-slash-bodyguard's voice, she rubbed her thumb over the smooth wooden disk one last time before putting it back in its drawer and locking it with a stream of her will. She'd spent a lifetime looking for the wand; it would keep until after she'd briefed Wilson on his next assignment.

Leader smoothed her short salt-and-pepper hair and grabbed a random file of no importance before pressing the button to reply. "Send him in."

She rose and began her pantomime routine when she heard LaSalle open her office door. "Fulcrum to see you," the brick of an assistant-slash-bodyguard informed her.

"Thank you, David. Fulcrum, take a seat. I'll be with you in a second," she addressed them as she placed the dummy file in a cabinet. In her periphery, she saw the door close behind LaSalle and Wilson sit in one of the oversized white leather chairs set at an angle to her massive desk.

Leader pulled the pertinent files and turned her piercing gray eyes on Wilson. Dressed in one of his bespoke suits, he sat calmly under her gaze. When her scan found him soundly Wilson and only Wilson, she took a seat in her high-backed office chair. "Thirty minutes ago, we got a call through the regular channels from the Minneapolis branch of the Institute of Tradition. Last night, they were performing a routine appeasement ritual when the flour moved on its own and spelled out 'Help'."

She pushed the folder in his direction, and Wilson leaned forward to receive it. "What do we have in place in Minneapolis?" he asked as he started flipping through the pages. He usually had time to review beforehand, but circumstances hadn't afforded him the luxury.

"We have a treaty with the ghost population established in the '80s. It's based on the Great British 1917 Pacification Treaty, but there's a copy of it in the background section if you want to review the particulars," she added as an aside.

"It's also where *The Way Things Were* is produced. The chief editor is Lisa Olson, but she isn't involved with the esoteric side of things. A practitioner oversees the rituals. Our normal contact is M'lissa Myer, but she's out of town. In her absence, her second led the appeasement ritual in her place and reported the incident."

Wilson skipped past the pages of area history and stopped

when he found the staff bios, matching faces with names. "Orhan?" he asked.

"That's correct," she affirmed.

"Two practitioners in the same branch?" Wilson commented at the rarity. Appeasement rituals didn't require practitioners to work, as long as the correct things were said and done.

"The area has a mixed history and a double homicide by a poltergeist prompted our initial involvement decades ago, which makes this sudden appeal more concerning. The ghosts are our allies in keeping worse things at bay," she explained in broad strokes.

"Parameters?" he asked in typical fashion. Leader always liked that Fulcrum got to the point and didn't need a lot of hand holding.

"We're sending you in as Damon Warwick to follow up on a reported supernatural phenomenon during the performance of a bequeathment stipulation."

He closed the file and gave her a curt nod. "Anything else I should know?"

Leader broke the bad news last. "It took place at the fairgrounds and the state fair started today."

The Minnesota State Fair was huge and boasted the largest daily attendance of any fair in the nation. Not only would he have to dodge tons of fairgoers during his investigation, but if something went FUBAR, the potential for causalities was high. The subtle change in his eyes told her he understood the implications.

"Got it. Can I stop by the sixth floor for provisions?"

"If you think that's necessary," Leader obliquely gave him permission while resting responsibility for the decision squarely on his shoulders. "You fly out tomorrow morning. David has your travel details." Her tone indicated she was done.

Wilson rose and buttoned his suit jacket. "Consider it done."

Just as he was about to leave, he heard his name. "Fulcrum, if you go to the sixth floor, will you check on Hans and see how he's settling in?"

He was momentarily thrown off kilter by the digression and the almost maternal nature of the request. There were few people she referred to by first name. Then he reminded himself of her interest in Hans. She'd taken great pains to accommodate his quirks to secure a second practitioner that could work magic with technology.

"I actually had lunch with him today. He seemed happy as a clam at high tide," he replied.

The contours of her face didn't change but she seemed pleased to him nonetheless. "Good travels, Fulcrum."

Wilson left her office and closed the door behind him. He went to drop the metaphysical bracing he'd always employed during meetings with Leader but found it was already gone. *Huh.* Sometime during the briefing, he must have unconsciously released it and the fact that he'd come out of it no worse for wear was both pleasing and puzzling.

Even though Leader was business as usual, Wilson was less certain about how to proceed after their time together in the Magh Meall. He'd witnessed her withstand some big magic and her girlish giggle was inextricably linked with the memory of Alberia's indescribable beauty and her perfect rainbow. It was the most he'd learned about his boss in over a decade, and he was at a loss of what to do with it.

"Are you okay?" LaSalle asked him when he noticed he hadn't moved from the door.

"Yeah, just thinking what a mess conducting an investigation at a state fair is going to be," he lied. "You have my itinerary?"

LaSalle handed him a stack of trifold papers. "Also sent to your email."

"Thanks. Mind helping me get down to the sixth floor?" Wilson asked as he tucked the pages into the file.

LaSalle raised an eyebrow. "I didn't allot any special equipment. What did you have in mind?"

"At the very least, a hag stone. The fair is a big place," Wilson argued. "Maybe some Babel lozenges if I'm going to be speaking with ghosts."

"For American ghosts?" LaSalle asked incredulously.

"*Minnesotan* ghosts," Wilson countered.

"Fair enough," LaSalle conceded. "Let me push a request down so Weber can get it ready. Maybe an hour, but it should be before end of day."

"Sounds good. I'll be in my office reading this," Wilson replied, tapping his index finger on the file.

He stopped by the break room on the fifth floor and grabbed an espresso in a can to stave off the afternoon sleepies before walking down the sloped hall to his office. He held his palm to the door pad and turned on the lights upon entry.

Once he was settled, he started with the account of what happened, as told by Orhan. Like magic, appeasement rituals were culturally dependent. Soothing American ghosts required different protocol than say European or Asian ghosts but the principle was the same: feed the spirits. The idea was to prevent the ghosts from getting metaphysically hungry through regular rituals.

It was rare to have the ghosts answer back in such a demonstrative way. Moving objects in the material world required less energy than manifesting, but it still took a considerable amount. It made him wonder if Orhan had infused the ritual with magic or if the ghost had called out *because* there was a practitioner present.

He flipped to Orhan's bio. According to his Minnesota driver's license, he was forty-seven years old, six feet seven inches tall, and weighed two hundred and two pounds. He'd worked at the Institute for fifteen years with previous publishing work experience. He was a registered magician who had done a little shoplifting as a kid, but otherwise had no record. Between his flowery description of the event and theatrical driver's license photo, he'd put money on Orhan being the kind of practitioner than owned more than one cape and spoke in British English during rituals.

Wilson moved on to the background of the location. Before the 322 acres in Ramsey County became the permanent site of the Minnesota State Fair in 1885, it was a poor farm. Akin to Dickensian workhouses, they were the American "solution" to poverty. Prior to state and federal intervention in social welfare, counties were responsible for their poor. Much of America was rural in the mid-nineteenth century, and it was impractical to keep the poor in centralized housing. Instead, they created working farms scattered across the countryside in which destitute residents were obligated to do the work that they could, depending on the state of their health.

At the time, pauperism was considered the outcome of moral turpitude and poor farms were bleak, spartan places at their best. At their worst, the near-complete authority the managers of the farm had over their residents led to exploitation and abuse. Such was the case with the poor farm upon which the Minnesota State Fair now stood.

By the time the brutality of the managers and staff was revealed, hundreds had already died, many of whom were interred in unmarked graves throughout the farmland. The scandal caused quite a stir and local politicians moved quickly to salvage the program. They consolidated all the county poor farm locations into a new custom-built site designed to be significantly more humane and sold the land to the fair in an attempt to break with its sordid past.

Politically, it had succeeded. The politicians were hailed as good Christians, and the well-to-do patted themselves on the back for helping the poor, even though they were still expected to do hard labor for the most basic of subsistence. Everyone loved going to the new fair, which grew and expanded with the population and its popularity. However, in the land of the dead, the victims did not forget so easily.

In 1910, the fair started expanding over the sites of the hidden unmarked graves and the ghosts found an audience to air their grievances. Fairgoers had reported cold spots, things moving or going missing, apparitions, and even two possessions. With the popularity of spiritualism, the hauntings only raised the fair's cachet. Within ten years, it had a reputation for spiritual activity and séance tents popped up like mushrooms. The "ghost craze" only lost steam when the Great Depression hit, and the ghosts could not compete with the endless hardships of the material world.

Even though the people of Minnesota had stopped seeking the ghosts out, their numbers rose year after year—as Wilson saw from the list of names and dates of death of known ghosts. The fair, like any long-running public event, had suffered a continuous series of tragedies: deaths of circus performers, deaths via livestock accidents, deaths via airshow accidents, deaths via mechanical ride failures, deaths by misadventure, a few actual murders, and quite a lot of people just naturally kicking the bucket due to age or known medical conditions. In total, there were thirty-two ghosts noted in the treaty, which didn't seem like a lot, but ask someone who's been in an area with that many active ghosts and they would say it was haunted as hell.

It made sense to Wilson. Dying in unexpected ways or environs had a tendency to create new residents in the land of the dead. It was part of the reason every culture had special customs around death—to let the spirit know it had died and it was time to move on. Or why hospitals were not nearly as haunted as movies would have you believe. Everyone going into the hospital knew people died at the hospital. But no one expected to die when they went to the fair. It was a location of merriment, a place of lights and laughter.

Postwar prosperity brought hope and life back to the country and the ghosts returned to the Minnesota State Fair with a vengeance. Paranormal reports steadily climbed through the '60s and '70s until a double murder in 1983 drew the Salt Mine's full attention. Two agents had been dispatched, the homicidal undead neutralized, and a treaty made between the ghost population and the Mine.

Wilson flipped through the treaty and recognized blocks of text as near-exact copies from the 1917 Pacification Treaty with the Missenden ghosts but with American spellings and clauses that were uniquely Minnesotan, such as starting the state fair with rye flour and ending it with a burnt offering of walleye.

As always, the names of the establishing agents were redacted, but whoever had done it had been sloppy. The black bars were not quite opaque and Wilson could just make out two names: Patron and Deacon.

Wilson sat up in his chair when he did the math. Patron was no surprise. He was solidly over the hill when he trained Wilson a little over a decade ago, but Deacon? Either he started working for the Mine as a teenager or he was quite a bit older than he claimed.

Wilson tucked it away as an interesting factoid before picking up his receiver and calling it in to LaSalle. Security protocol was only as good as its weakest link. While the sloppy redaction hadn't caused any damage in this situation, who knew what could happen the next time?

Chapter Four

Minneapolis, Minnesota, USA
28th of August, 6:35 a.m. (GMT-5)

Richard Orhan picked up the phone and dialed work. It had been a long night, but he had made it through to sunrise. He pressed Olson's extension as soon as the recording picked up. "You've reached Lisa Olson, chief editor of *The Way Things Were*. I'm out of my office. Please leave a brief message with your name and number, and I'll return your call."

He waited for the beep before speaking. "Hello, Lisa…this is Richard. I apologize for the short notice, but could you arrange for someone else to meet with the Detroit representative? I'm coming down with something and I won't be at the office today. Thanks for your help in this matter, and I'll see you on Monday." He ended the call and put his phone back on the desk.

He was exhausted—mentally, physically, and emotionally. He'd had panic attacks all his life but never one this bad. They started when he was a kid after watching *Poltergeist* at a sleepover, and they only got worse when he discovered his ability to practice magic. Up until then, he'd believed adults when they told him that monsters were just figments of his imagination, but if magic was real, why not monsters?

He initially chalked up his anxiety to the upcoming meeting with the auditor from Detroit. Myer usually took care of these things, and he just followed the instructions she'd left in the binder before she'd left for her month in Europe. He had no idea they would send someone the next day.

He'd worked late into the night covering his tracks, but instead of easing his troubled mind, it got worse. It ramped up after midnight just as he was putting away his work. His mind ran an endless cycle of doom, and his heart rate rose with each iteration. He was intimately familiar with the incipient signs of a panic attack by now, but unlike his younger self, he had tools to cope with them.

He methodically went through the house, making sure the doors and windows were closed and locked and the wards intact. He cleared each room by turning on all the lights and opening all the interior doors to reinforce that there was nothing hiding in the closets and dark corners. Talking himself through physically securing his environment was often enough to break the anxiety gyre, but not this time. His heart was still racing and his breathing became ever more rapid and shallow.

Finally, he broke down and took his abortive medication, the ones that were supposed to put the brakes on a panic attack, and started his breathing exercises. He knew if he could slow his breath, his heart rate would follow. As the waves of dread broke over him, he repeated a personal mantra he'd developed over the years: *I am safe. I am bedrock. Nothing can move me.* As a practitioner, he was better attuned to his will than most, and the melding of behavioral therapy, biofeedback, and medical assistance had seen him through to the morning.

Now that he'd contacted work, he could rest. Monsters couldn't get you during the day. Night was their domain. He crawled into bed fully clothed with his keys and wallet in his pocket. It was yet another measure he took to calm his mind, the knowledge that he was prepared to escape at a moment's notice.

He pulled the covers all the way up to his chin. Their heft was comforting and it felt terribly cold for August. He closed his eyes and focused on the rise of his chest with each breath as he drifted into unconsciousness, but his eyes snapped open when a high-pitched squeak broke the quiet. He identified it immediately: the closet door.

He watched in terror as it slowly opened on its own. In the early light seeping in through the window, he could see his clothes move on the hangers. *There is nothing in the closet*, he told himself, but he couldn't stop his pounding heart.

A spike of fear pinned him to the bed. Even though the sun was rising, the closet was growing darker. The metal hangers scraped against the rod as they parted, and the grating noise broke him out of his paralysis. In a manic frenzy, he hurled his will against the darkness and pushed back the covers as he leapt out of bed. He could see his quickened breath pluming in front of him as he ran for the bedroom door and yanked it open.

Out from the closet stepped a clown with long red and white striped arms and legs. Its frizzy red hair poofed from under its royal blue cap that tapered to a lone bell. It jingled as it moved along with the bells on the points of its shiny silver jester's collar and the ones on its comical shoes.

The sound transfixed Orhan and he couldn't stop himself. He had to look. He glanced over his shoulder and saw a life-sized version of the clown doll from *Poltergeist*. Its wide smile taunted him as it filled him with fear. Color drained from the world, starting at the edges of his vision and moving inward. The cold became unbearable as everything turned gray, and the last splash of color Orhan saw was the candy apple red of the clown's nose.

*****

Elijah Jenkin made a detour to the Institute of Tradition on his way to the fair after getting Olson's message. She was light on the details, but he could tell by her tone it was urgent. Her office door was open, but he paused at the threshold and knocked on the frame all the same. The matriarch of the magazine stopped her typing and raised her hazel eyes off the screen.

"Oh good, you're here," she greeted him and waved him

in. As he sat in one of the chairs opposite her desk, she took her readers off and gave the younger man her full attention. "Richard called in sick and I need someone to show whoever Detroit is sending around the fair. I'd do it, but I've got to get the next issue ironed out for the printers before the weekend."

He guessed where this was going. "And you figured, 'why not Elijah? He's already going to be there running the booth.'"

The older women brushed back her gray hair from her eyes and pointed a friendly finger at him. "That's why I like you, quick on the uptake."

He grinned "Who are they sending?"

"No clue, but I've arranged tickets and passes." She dug around her desk and handed him an envelope. "Just show them around, be congenial, and roll with the punches," she advised her junior. Olson knew what she was talking about; she'd managed to sustain a career in what many considered a dying industry and she was only two years from retirement, if she chose to take it.

Jenkin opened the envelope and double checked the contents. "Any idea why they're coming?"

"Richard said something about it yesterday afternoon," she said vaguely. "Don't quote me on this, but I think there is interest in the phenomenon that happened a few nights ago."

"Ah, that makes sense!" Jenkin replied. There were believers in the organization as well as their readership. "Give me a second to check in on the booth and let them know the situation," he said as he pulled out his phone. Olson gestured for him to proceed and he stepped into the hall.

His crew knew they were opening without him but assumed he would be joining them later. He had no idea how long he would have to babysit the person from the Detroit branch, and if they wanted to see the booth, he wouldn't be stopping by alone.

He knew better than to call. No one answered their phones these days and some never even bothered to set up their voicemail. He tapped out a message with his thumbs and got an immediate "*k*."

He was putting his phone back in his pocket when a small man approached him. "Excuse me, I'm looking for Richard Orhan. I stopped by his office but no one was there." He was thin and clean-shaven with brown eyes and short brown hair showing the first hints of gray, but the thing that stuck out to Jenkin was his attire. Dressed in an impeccable blue suit and blue and gold houndstooth silk tie with a leather attaché case in hand, he was hardly fair-ready. Jenkin wondered if their wires got crossed or if Orhan had another appointment he'd forgotten to cancel.

"Are you the person from the Detroit branch?" he ventured.

Wilson politely smiled. "Yes. Damon Warwick," he introduced himself and extended his hand.

Jenkin immediately recognized the name and plastered a warm smile on his face. Warwick was the elusive executive who held the purse strings and the final voice in any internal dispute or petition. He didn't attend the board meetings and wasn't in any of the group photographs, but every branch knew his name.

"Dr. Elijah Jenkin," the younger man reciprocated and Wilson recalled his details from the briefing. "Richard is out sick so I'll be showing you around, but let's stop in and say hi to Lisa first."

Jenkin led the way and cleared his throat to get her attention. "Lisa, Damon Warwick from Detroit has arrived," he stated the name deliberately. It dropped like a brick through a glass pane window—the Comptroller and Auditor General of the Institute of Tradition was about to enter her office.

Only the weight of Olson's thick wooden chair saved it from being knocked over from the speed of her rise. "Mr. Warwick, so nice to finally meet you!" she greeted him like she'd expected him all along. "Lisa Olson, chief editor."

"I understand Mr. Orhan isn't feeling well?" Wilson indirectly asked for more information.

"Yes, he sends his apologies," she fibbed. "He called this morning sick as a dog, but Elijah knows the fair like the back of his hand. He's been in charge of our booth for years and he attended the pre-opening bequeathment request," she answered smoothly. "Please, take a seat. Would you like a drink?" she asked and motioned to the chairs.

"No, thank you," Wilson politely declined while remaining

standing. "If it's all the same to you, I'd like to get to the fairgrounds as quickly as possible."

"Certainly, Mr. Warwick. Would you like to ride with me or drive yourself?" Jenkin asked.

Wilson considered the pros and cons of each before answering. "Perhaps a ride this first time would be prudent, Dr. Jenkin. That way you could show me the exact location where the alleged contact was made."

Jenkin wondered if Warwick was a believer or a skeptic, but his expression and turn of phrase was too neutral to tell. While his mind chewed on the question, his smiling face betrayed nothing. "That sounds fine. My car's in the garage. And please, call me Elijah."

The two men took the measure of each other over pleasantries about Wilson's flight, the weather, and Jenkin's role at the Institute on the way to the car—Jenkin had no way of knowing how much Wilson already knew about him. While Jenkin drew from his anthropology background, Wilson probed him with his will, confirming that Jenkin was not a practitioner.

"So, how much do you know about the fair?" Jenkin asked broadly when they hit traffic.

"Some, but not a lot. The basics," Wilson succinctly answered. Jenkin fought the urge to sigh. *This is going to be a long car ride.* "Would it be possible to hear your account of what happened with the rye flour?"

Seeing an opportunity to fill the considerable time they'd have until they reached vendor parking, Jenkin began talking, adding as much detail as he could remember. Wilson listened carefully, nodding every so often. Jenkin spoke naturally, with ease, and it matched what Orhan had reported. Wilson asked a few questions and when Jenkin confirmed Orhan's story without repeating the exact same phrases, Wilson crossed "magically induced memory" off the list.

Jenkin drove through the gates and eventually found a parking space. "Is this the parking lot where it occurred?" Wilson inquired.

"Sorry, no. I should have warned you to change into sneakers. We've got a lot of walking before we get there. The lot where it happened is only for agricultural use," Jenkin replied apologetically.

"No problem. These are more comfortable than they look," Wilson reassured him and allowed a small smile to slip out. "Any chance we'll pass a corn dog stand from here to there? They never taste right when you try to make them at home."

Jenkin grinned. "I can do you one better. Ever tried a Pronto Pup?" Wilson shook his head. "It's a Minnesota State Fair staple. Just don't let anyone hear you call them 'corn dogs' or we may end up chased out of town."

He led him through the crowds to the nearest vendor and after a ten-minute wait, they acquired their battered "Banquet on a Stick" and headed south.

Seeing the terse, suited man nosh on deep-fried meat on the stick humanized him in Jenkin's mind and he mustered the courage to ask what he'd been toying with since they met. "Let me ask you something…" he eased into the question. "Have you ever experienced anything like that?"

"Like what?" Wilson played dumb. He nibbled off the crusty bits at the end of the stick and wiped his mouth and hands before tossing his trash into the bin.

"The supernatural. Ghosts. Stuff moving by itself," Jenkin elaborated.

Based on his narrative, Wilson pegged him as a skeptical believer and answered accordingly. "A couple of times, but I don't make a habit of attributing everything that's strange to spirits." He saw a look of relief on Jenkin's face in his peripheral vision. Everyone wanted to find a kindred spirit. "What about you? Do you think you witnessed a genuine supernatural event?"

Jenkin wasn't sure how to answer. During his academic training, he'd never been "a believer." As a person of science and reason, his interest in religious, spiritual, occult, and magical beliefs was from an anthropological perspective. He saw belief in the supernatural as a coping strategy created by a sentient species that found the idea of random creation and factual purposelessness untenable.

Such ideas still held strong sway over humanity, much to modernists' chagrin, although he had enough social skills to avoid being *that* guy—the killjoy compelled to point out that traditions people hung their hopes and joys on were manufactured, mutually agreed upon artifice. But what was humanity if not hairless monkeys who had traded their tail for bigger brains only to end up with anxiety? However, he couldn't dismiss the possibility that it could be real. He'd witnessed and experienced too many things that defied explanation since starting at the Institute.

"If you had asked me that question six years ago, I would still be looking for the wires, so to speak," Jenkin replied cautiously. "But yes, I think something that cannot be explained with traditional science happened. I don't know what it was, but it was something."

They turned the corner from the Haunted Mansion and Jenkin stopped at the edge of the gravel parking lot. "And we've made it to Ag parking," he announced for Wilson's benefit, if the smell of animals wasn't enough of a tip-off. Jenkin pointed to the northern-most section that was concrete. "We were over there on the paved part."

"I'd like to see the exact spot," Wilson pressed.

Jenkin obliged and led Wilson around the trucks and trailers. The smell of hay and manure strengthened as they walked deeper into the parking lot. He stopped next to a long steel trailer. "Right here."

"You're sure?"

Jenkin nodded. "You don't forget something like that."

Wilson started pacing the area. "Excellent. I think that's all I need for now. You can go ahead to the booth. I'm sure they'll appreciate having you back," he dismissed Jenkin.

Jenkin was at a loss for words. He'd assumed he would be out showing Warwick around for most of the day. "Uh, okay. If you're sure. Do you need a lift back?"

"No, thank you. I'll get a taxi," Wilson declined the offer as he crouched and looked under the trailer.

Jenkin pulled out an envelope from his pocket. "These are for you, and there's a parking pass in there as well as a map."

Wilson accepted the packet and spooled out a little will. "Thank you, Elijah. You've been very helpful."

Jenkin smiled and dreamily walked to the booth. The ramp-up to the fair was always a stressful time and he suddenly felt more at ease than he'd felt in days. For a brief moment, he felt like order had been restored, with a place for everything and everything in its place.

Chapter Five

Falcon Heights, Minnesota, USA
28th of August, 12:15 p.m. (GMT-5)

As soon as Jenkin was out of view, Wilson pulled out his vape pen and transformed it into a saltcaster by rotating the end until the notches lined up. He brought it to his lips and blew out a distribution of fine salt before flipping it back to a vape pen. Most visitors to the fair today had already unloaded their animals, but there was a small and steady stream of people crossing the lot for various reasons. Even though salt casting only took a little more than a minute, no less than three people crossed his line of sight.

He pulled out his phone and pretended to scroll while vaping to help sell the ruse. When the salt remained in its even distribution, he had his answer: Orhan had not done any magic during the ritual. Whoever sent the message did so on their own power, which led Wilson to one conclusion: he needed to talk to the ghosts.

Holding a séance wasn't difficult, but the conditions were less than ideal. First, it was the middle of the day, which made it significantly harder for ghosts to manifest...but that was unavoidable given the urgency of the situation. Second, trying to find a private location near the initial call for help was going to be tricky. Even with the maze of tall animal trailers, he didn't want to risk being seen. Additionally, there was the added irritation of Orhan's absence. The only magician that might have been able to shed some light on what actually happened had bailed at the last minute.

He brushed his shoe across the enchanted salt and dispersed the magic as he looked for a suitable place to hold a séance. He checked the back of the buildings north of the parking lot without any luck. He considered using a room in the Haunted Mansion, but that had even more traffic than the parking lot. Momentarily stumped, he walked back into the throng of people in the fairgrounds proper for something farther afield down the long crowded street. Even though the search was a bust, it certainly smelled better than the trailers.

The trailers! he scolded himself. He didn't need to scour the premises for a private room. There were literally dozens of mobile sheds with doors that could be secured within a stone's throw of the site of the appeasement ritual. All he needed to do was to find one with solid siding and high vents to prevent people on the outside from looking in. As he returned to the agricultural parking lot, he added "minimal dung" to the list of criteria.

He moved from trailer to trailer until he found a suitable candidate. He popped the Masterlock No. 3 with a wave rake lock pick in under three seconds; the best-selling locks always made his job easier. Once inside the solid powder white aluminum walls, he grabbed the muck shovel from the storage area and scraped the droppings to one side. *At least I didn't wear my good shoes.* Then he laid down a series of animal blankets over the floor. It was far from clean, but at least he could sit without staining his suit.

To make sure he wasn't interrupted, he zip-tied the interior of the doors and got to work. He placed and lit six tea lights in a circle and sat on the cleanest section of the blankets. He popped a Babel lozenge out of its blister pack. The olivine tablet slowly melted under his tongue, allowing him to communicate with ghosts despite differences in language or slang for a brief time. The taste—now in spearmint—had certainly improved since the prototype.

When it had completely dissolved, he summoned his will, pushing it out in a circular motion. Once he established a steady vortex of power for ghosts to manifest, he spoke softly in the rhythm to his swirling will. "Spirits of the fair, your plea for help has been heard. Come into my circle and be met by a friend." Even though it was barely a whisper in the trailer, his will amplified his words and they ripped out through the land of the dead like rocks dropping into still water.

It didn't take long for one of the candles to flicker, and Wilson flattened his voice to welcome his visitor. "To the spirit who has arrived, my greet—"

"About damn time you got here!" a gruff male voice echoed in the trailer. "With allies like you, who need enemies?!"

"My apologies for the delay," Wilson said diplomatically. "I'm here to help now. Be edified and tell me what's wrong." He cut off the thread of his will and let it circle into oblivion for the spirit to consume and manifest.

The ghost slurped Wilson's will like a string of spaghetti and a translucent figure dressed in combat gear with a holstered M1911 at his side appeared. He spitfired syllables in a raw staccato, "We don't have time for pleasantries! Thompson, Jones, and Harmon just went down. Brand and Gilford before that. Bunny's also missing. I haven't seen her in a week. I assume it got her." Wilson recognized the names as ghosts from the treaty.

"Lieutenant Colonel Haughton?" Wilson made a guess. Haughton was an Army Air Force officer that had fought in the Pacific theater and worked as a stunt pilot when the war was over. An engine failure during a dive had claimed his life and the life of Bunny Montgomery, the young woman who'd been his wing walker.

"Of course it's me, you jackass! I've been hiding for weeks, fighting and retreating, and you think you're clever just by telling me my own name?!"

The ghost's insults rolled over Wilson as he focused on getting information out of him. "Who are you fighting?"

"I don't know. Our numbers were already low from the

wackadoodles picking us off one by one, but then one night a shadowy figure started stalking us. I watched it swallow a whole squad in one go. I haven't seen anyone else in days. I think I'm the only one left."

The magic of the lozenge translated and Wilson understood his meaning. Magicians had been hunting them and there was only reason practitioners needed ghosts: to power magical items. It was one of the protections the Salt Mine was supposed to ensure under the treaty. But the shadowy figure was a mystery to Wilson. He wasn't aware of anything that ate ghosts, other than other ghosts, of course, but Haughton would have recognized a fellow ghost.

"I promise I'll get to the bottom of this," was what Wilson said, but the magic of the lozenge translated it to: *Buck up, soldier. Reinforcements have arrived.* The ghost held himself a little taller after the pep talk. He wasn't sure how good the small fry sitting in front of him would be in a fistfight, but he figured him to be one hell of a wackadoodle. Haughton's gas tank hadn't been this full in ages and he'd just had one sliver of the shrimp's will.

"Tell me more about these practitioners," Wilson prompted him. "Maybe they know something about this shadow."

"There's only one, and he's one of yours," Haughton warned him. "The tall one with the funny looking beard, not the pretty blonde with the nice gams. You've got a rotten apple in your bunch."

The description sounded a whole lot like Richard Orhan, but Wilson asked a follow-up question for confirmation. "Same one that was there when you sent out the SOS?"

"Ironic, ain't it?" Haughton said sarcastically. "Figure he couldn't deny it with all those witnesses." His smirk suddenly disappeared and he drew his weapon. "It's here!" he yelled as he fired the ethereal gun. The M1911 kept going well after the eight-round maximum, aimed at something in the land of the dead well beyond the walls of the trailer.

In the blink of an eye, augmented Wilson was on his feet, Glock 26 drawn. He scanned the metaphysical landscape for a target. "I don't see it."

"Useless bastard! It's right there!" the ghostly lieutenant colonel shrieked as he unloaded a few more rounds.

An absolutely black human hand appeared out of the white aluminum siding of the trailer and reached for Haughton. It hurt Wilson's eyes to look at it. It was like staring into the sun except instead of being too bright, it was the absolute absence of light itself.

"Do something!" the ghost howled as he scrambled to elude the grasping figure. More of the shadow's humanoid form entered the trailer to claim its prey. Wilson's gun was loaded with banishment bullets and he made sure to aim downward; if it didn't banish the shadow, it wouldn't fly through the parking lot and into a passerby outside.

He squeezed the trigger and the 9mm chunked a hole into

the trailer's wooden floorboards, sending bits of hay and manure flying along with splinters of wood. The inscribed runes along the side of the bullet didn't banish the creature, but it did get its attention. The blackness turned its head toward Wilson, noticing him for the first time. Haughton saw his opportunity and broke from the mortal realm. As he fled, Wilson dropped the vortex just in case the shadow had any ideas of using it as a power source.

This didn't look like any shadow demon he'd fought before and he didn't know what to expect, but he knew the more time he bought Haughton, the farther away he could get. With the séance over, Wilson reclaimed the full strength of his will and puffed out his chest, metaphysically speaking. His veins coursed with adrenaline and augmentation magic.

The shadow responded to the challenge and in its blackness, blinking lights started twinkling like stars in the night sky. The change and contrast drew Wilson's eye. In a flash, he saw images of himself as a child holding his father's hand as they walked down the midway at the Northern Idaho State Fair. It was a memory long buried and forgotten, but he knew it to be genuinely his.

Even though the shadow had no facial features, Wilson felt the creature smile before it jumped outside of the trailer in pursuit of its ghostly quarry. He flew to the end of the trailer and snapped the zip-tie with his augmented strength. The bright afternoon sun stung after staring into the unending black. He jumped into the parking lot and searched for signs of the shadow, but it was gone.

He holstered his gun and quickly reentered the trailer, closing the doors behind him. He needed to vacate the area in case anyone had heard the gunfire, but not before salt casting. He pulled out his vape pen and blew the fine grains in the shadow's path. The salt started to dance, forming a pattern Wilson hadn't seen before. He snapped a picture on his phone and quickly returned the shovel and blankets to the narrow storage area in the front of the trailer. Except for the hole in the floor and the shoveled dung, he left everything as he'd found it and returned to the fairgrounds.

Once he was lost in the crowd, he tried to make sense of everything. If Haughton was the only one left of the thirty-two ghosts named in the treaty, that was a whole lot of magical mojo recently crammed into items, which suggested the most obvious motive was money. There was a steady demand for enchanted goods in the magical community and they fetched high prices.

It put a whole new angle on Orhan's no-show this morning: wait to pillage until the only other practitioner at the Institute was on an extended vacation—a four-week tour of Europe and North Africa with her significant other, according to Jenkin. He pulled out his phone and immediately sent the Mine an update along with the shadow figure's magical signature and a request for additional information on Orhan, including financials. He chose to leave out his memories from the report. Those were private and once he knew what he was dealing with, he'd take care of it himself.

He oriented himself and headed to the taxi stand to pick up his rental at the Institute's office. It was time to have a proper sit-down with Richard Orhan.

Chapter Six

Wilson was on route to Kenwood, a well-to-do neighborhood of Minneapolis when his phone beeped at him. He pulled the rental car over immediately and checked his phone. *Exercise caution. Do not return to fair. Meet Deacon arriving on flight DL1594 20:20.*

He reread the message and considered the implications. If Deacon was on his way, they got a hit on the signature and it's bad. Real bad. Deacon was the oldest and most experienced Salt Mine agent and his specialty was undead, which would explain why the banishment bullet didn't work. It wasn't a shadow demon, but some type of incorporeal undead Wilson didn't recognize. *Exercise caution* was either redundant or a signal that the danger exceeded the level implicit in bringing in Deacon. Considering only Leader or LaSalle would have added it to the message, he was inclined to believe the latter.

He looked at the groomed suburban landscape over the dashboard as his car idled. He was slightly annoyed that they hadn't sent any information about what the creature was, but

Deacon would be here soon enough with answers. The question now was how to proceed.

Wilson was only a few blocks away from Richard Orhan's house. He could turn back and wait for Deacon's arrival, but it seemed a waste. All he would do was wait in a hotel room for hours, and his encounter in the trailer had convinced him Haughton was right. Time was of the essence. He confirmed he'd received the message and indicated his intention of following up with Orhan. After all, they had only warned him off returning to the fair.

He drove past Orhan's corner house three times from different directions, scanning the area. It was a sprawling two-story affair with a manicured lawn and a well-maintained flower bed neatly squared off by a low fence whose purpose was entirely decorative. Unlike some of the other houses, it sat on a large lot and outshined all the other homes, which was quite a feat in this neighborhood. He wondered how Orhan could afford such a place on his salary. The Institute paid well, but not that well.

He didn't see any movement in the windows and parked a few houses down and across the street. First, he called Orhan's listed home number, but there was no answer. Then he tried his cell, but it went to voicemail.

Wilson exited his rental with his attaché case and walked across the street, taking advantage of the shadow of a large tree to shield himself from the warm sun. On his approach, he threaded out his will to see if there were any wards on the wrought iron gate at the front of the yard. He found two: one against faeries and one against ghosts. He passed through and stepped onto the covered porch. There were more wards on the house, including an alarm ward.

To Wilson's expert eye, they were slapdash in quality and organization, a dilettante's effort at best, but that wasn't what Wilson came for. He wanted to know how good Orhan was at capturing ghosts and entrapping them in enchanted items. The fact that he had this much magical security in place suggested a practitioner of some ability with something to protect. *Or hide*, he added.

He rang the doorbell and waited, but no one answered. He rang again, and when he got the same response, he went around the house and peered into a recently-attached detached garage. A shiny late model Honda was inside. It was possible that Orhan was inside and sleeping heavily enough to ignore two phone calls and a double doorbell, but Wilson found it unlikely.

He walked to the backyard and found no electronic security in place. He didn't like risking his Institute of Tradition alias on a break-in, but if Orhan was caught abducting ghosts and putting them into items, that was more than enough leverage for Wilson to get him to forget about illegal entry into his home. Still, there was no need to tip his hand.

Wilson sent out a thread of will, snaking it counterclockwise around the house until it encircled the entire structure. Once it returned to him, he started vibrating the thread at various frequencies trying to find just the right combination and sequence that would snap Orhan's magical alarm wards without triggering them. It was the magical equivalent of raking a mundane lock.

After a minute, he felt a metaphysical pop of the wards give way. *A whole minute?* Wilson thought as he reeled in his will. *Maybe Orhan is better than I'd given him credit.*

Wilson entered and quietly closed the door behind him. He listened but heard nothing stir except for the swinging pendulum of a grandfather clock somewhere in the house. Nonetheless, he readied his will and proceeded with caution.

The interior wasn't anything like what he'd expected: it reeked of little old lady. The decor was expensive and high quality, but at least thirty years out of date. Any potentially empty space was crammed with frilly bits and bobs, ranging from cute knickknacks to luxury bobbles. The walls were decorated with nice paintings and dated family pictures. It wasn't hard to pick out Orhan from the pack: even as a kid, he towered over everyone.

Drawing his Glock, he edged past the kitchen and found the door to the basement along the short hall. Wilson left it for last, wanting to secure the rest of the house before going into a space with only one exit.

Just past the grandfather clock was the entrance into the

living room. Some of the décor had been changed to join the twenty-first century, namely a large leather sectional and a massive TV that dominated the room. Before it were three different console systems with only one controller attached to each.

In the next room was a proper sitting room with a baby grand piano. The couch and chairs were placed around a coffee table upon which sat a stack of oversized art books. He moved on to the stairwell.

The steps were carpeted, but Wilson wasn't lulled into a false sense of security. Stairwells were universally the noisiest part of the house. He listened at the bottom before ascending, but heard no sound from the upper story.

He wasn't entirely surprised when he found the body on the landing at the top of the stairs. *Damn, he's tall*, Wilson thought as he approached. Even though he was lying face down, Wilson had no doubt it was Orhan: his torso and most of his thighs were on the wide landing, and his calves were *still* in the room.

"Mr. Orhan, are you all right?" he asked before getting any closer. While he waited for a reply, he did a quick visual sweep of the room where Orhan's feet lay. There were no signs of an altercation, and everything was neat and orderly except for the unmade bed.

Wilson crouched down and reached for his neck to see if there was a pulse. When his fingers had almost contacted Orhan's skin, Wilson reflexively pulled them back. The body was cold. Real cold. Colder than dry ice.

Wilson immediately backed away and aimed his gun at Orhan's body. He cautiously nudged it with his foot and it was solid like a log. It didn't give an inch. If Orhan called in this morning and died after that, it was well within the window of rigor mortis, but this obviously went beyond that. The body was stuck to the carpet despite the fact there was no visible blood. He tested the fibers just around the body to confirm his suspicions: Orhan was literally frozen to the carpet.

Why isn't he steaming? Wilson wondered as he stepped around the body. *Something this cold should be condensing the nearby water vapor.* The lack of trailing vapor left little doubt in Wilson's mind that the death was supernatural.

He holstered his weapon to salt cast the body. The range allowed him to keep a safe distance, and if this corpse wanted to pull a "not dead yet," he'd hear the ripping of the carpet long before he was in danger. The salt shook out into two distinct patterns, both of which Wilson recognized. The first was Orhan's signature from the briefing. The second was from the trailer.

Wilson was confused. Haughton had pegged the shadow as a ghost eater, and the fact that it didn't come at Wilson led him to believe it didn't have any interest in humans, but clearly, he was wrong.

He secured the second-floor rooms and confirmed there wasn't an attic and doubled back to the basement, which was empty and freshly painted in gray: the hallmark of recent water remediation. Satisfied the house was clear, he holstered his weapon and returned to Orhan's bedroom. He sent the Mine a message to let them know Orhan was dead, killed by the same thing he'd encountered in the trailer. Then he started his search.

The master suite was spacious, and it looked like Orhan used it as both a bedroom and an office. There were more paintings and pictures on the wall, but the modern self-assembly bookshelves sandwiched between them caught Wilson's attention. They were loaded with hundreds of modern occult and esoteric books. As mass published works, they held little arcane value, but it gave him an insight into Orhan's interests.

There was an old-fashioned queen-sized bed in a slightly recessed nook, and opposite the bed was a large desk with a laptop in the center and an antique apothecary's cabinet to one side. Tucked in the corner next to the desk was a glass curio case with a mixed selection of fine wares and vintage Americana.

This looks promising, Wilson thought as he retrieved the hag stone from the small, custom-made interior breast pocket he had added to all his suits for carrying such items. The stone was smooth to the touch, polished both by the water erosion that made it and the countless hands that had held it over the years. He lined up his eye with the hole in its center and immediately started counting. *One…two…three…*

The world went two-dimensional and lost its color

and vibrancy, as if the world had turned into an old sepia photograph. However, the items on an entire shelf of the curio lit up in bright hues against the dull background. He turned and swept the rest of the room and found nothing else magical except for a pen on the bookshelf inset into the headboard of the bed.

He pulled the hag stone away from his eye before he'd reached seven. He had ten seconds to sweep the room for magic before any real risk of thinning the barrier between realms, but he cut it shorter than that in light of the warning the Mine had issued.

That's a hell of a lot of enchanted items, he thought as he put the stone away. The majority were rings and necklaces, but there were also two crystal animal figures and something called "The Syco-Slate, the pocket fortune teller," the cylindrical precursor to the Magic 8-Ball. *Someone had a sense of humor*, he thought wryly.

Enchanted items had to be powered and there were a couple of ways to accomplish this. Usually, it was done with the concentrated and sequestered will of the item's creator, like the mushrooms Wilson had made for the hamadryad. Making magical items this way was karmically expensive compared to casting a spell because practitioners effectively had to preload them with all the magic before they were functional. Makers that were not wealthy had to spread out the creation over a long period of time to make the karmic debt manageable, like arcane layaway. Some tried to game the system and make items in the Magh Meall to circumvent karma, but that came with its own cost. Magic was never truly free.

Practitioners with the right knowledge and ability could trap ghosts into items and use their residual existence and connection with the land of the dead as the power source. Karmically it was a lot less expensive because the only cost was the magic used to trap the ghost and form the spell of the item, but the practice was morally questionable to say the least. Among modern practitioners, it was like the poor farms—a regrettable practice that was done in the past, but now we know better.

Wilson checked the case for wards and opened the doors of the curio when he found none. He ran his will over the items and none of them registered as malevolent. He cursed under his breath when those that contained ghosts felt smooth and worn to his will. If Orhan had powered any of these recently with the Minnesota State Fair ghosts, they would feel rough or raw. Any ghosts in these items had been there a while, although he couldn't date when they were made. It was like being able to tell the difference between green wood and dried wood, but once the wood was dry, there was no accurate way to know when it was cut. He'd bag and tag them later for the sake of completeness, but they weren't the items he was looking for.

He went to the bed and checked the fountain pen—no ghosts inside—and found a collection of leatherbound books next to it, a few of which had no titles. Because they didn't register as magic through the hag stone, he felt safe touching them and started with the blank spines. Before people titled spines, they used to ink the name of the work on the fore-edges, harkening back to a time when books were shelved flat with spines inward instead of out.

His heart skipped a beat when he saw *Daemonologie* in old, faded ink along the fore-edge. He flipped to the end of the book; instead of the *Newes from Scotland* pamphlet, it ended with Doctor Fian's long description of the various rituals of summoning and capturing ghosts to power magic wands.

Daemonologie was originally published in 1599, and its content captured the obsession of the time but was otherwise completely bunk. Because of its popularity, it was reprinted in 1603 with a limited number containing the instructions on how to actually capture ghosts to power enchanted items—essentially as a giant middle finger to King James and his support for the witch hunts sweeping England.

The *Expanded Daemonologie* was on the Mine's ALWAYS RETREIVE list. Restricting access to the work was one of the methods it used to protect the ghosts with whom they have treaties. Because they were aggressively rounded up and destroyed, they were rather rare. Wilson had only seen three, and one of them was in the Mine's library. Yet somehow, Orhan had gotten his hands on it. As far as Wilson was concerned, this gave Orhan the means along with the previously established opportunity and the ubiquitous motive of money, even if he seemed to be already doing well for himself. Often those who needed it the least were willing to take the greatest risks to get more.

Wilson was no stranger to old leather books, and this one had the look and feel of being recently rebound. He flipped through the pages for clues of its provenance and determined that the pages were also new, albeit quality craftsmen paper. This wasn't an original with a new skin. It was a facsimile done in the style of the time. He looked for maker's marks and found an inscription on the bottom of the page opposite the title page. "This Copy Produced by Triangle Book & Binding."

He sent another message with a request for information to the Mine, this one marked URGENT. Someone was making new copies of the *Expanded Daemonologie* and he needed to know who he was dealing with.

Chapter Seven

Minneapolis-Saint Paul International Airport, Minnesota, USA
28th of August, 8:42 p.m. (GMT-5)

Clarence Morris—codename Deacon—scanned the packed thoroughfare for the short, small man who was supposed to meet him. It took a while, but he eventually spotted him partially obscured behind a curvy beauty with whom he'd much rather rendezvous.

The stocky black man carefully picked his way through the throng and approached his target. "Mr. Warwick," he said, using Wilson's Institute of Tradition cover identity. Morris didn't have a professional background in tradecraft, but he was an old hand at remembering who was supposed to be whom, including himself. Today, he was Cedric Moore, longtime contributor to *The Way Things Were*.

"Mr. Moore," Wilson responded in kind and they shook hands like business associates. "How was your flight?"

"Considering it was the only time I wasn't getting more bad news from you, it was all right," Morris joked.

Wilson led the way to short-term parking and the suited pair fell into step—Morris pulling his standard-issue Salt Mine luggage and holding his black leather medical bag in the other hand and Wilson with his Korchmar Monroe attaché. Wilson's suit was more expensive and finer cut, but Morris wore his better. You couldn't buy swagger.

When they were safely in Wilson's rental, Morris took off his hat and addressed the younger agent directly. "I'm going to be straight with you. There are a lot of moving parts and this could turn into a right shit show if we don't handle it correctly. I need you to follow my lead one hundred percent if we are going to defuse the situation." It wasn't unusual for Morris to take lead when he was brought into another agent's case, but he felt it was best to set the tone from the get-go. There wasn't any room for error on this one.

Wilson nodded as he started the engine and cranked up the air conditioning. "Understood."

Morris reached into his pocket and produced a sealed manila envelope. "When you notified us about Orhan's death, I requested the Mine work on a distributed alarm system for the remaining Institute of Tradition employees that were at the appeasement ritual."

"There wasn't any casting done during the ritual," Wilson countered. "Do you think just being there puts them in danger?"

"It's a possibility," Morris answered as he fished out one of the thin plastic cards and held it between thumb and index finger. "These are the new Institute employee IDs. Hans has been working on integrating magic in magnetic strips and was able to modify these before I left. It won't offer any protection, but if necromantic energy comes within a hundred feet, it will trigger a proximity alarm keyed to you and me. I'm putting you in charge of distribution and response. I'm going to have my hands full." He slipped the card back into the envelope and handed it to Wilson.

He tucked it into his pocket for safe keeping. "I have a list of who attended the ritual, but it's going to be difficult to disseminate it to everyone until Monday. No one is going to be at the office on the opening weekend of the fair. The best I can do before Monday is stop by their booth and give them to the guy running it to distribute to the rest of his crew."

"Partial coverage is better than none," Morris replied.

"Where to first?"

"The fairgrounds," Morris answered immediately. "I need to assess how serious it is. We'll start where you held your séance and go from there. Then I want to see Orhan's body."

Wilson put the car into gear and followed the signs to the exit. "Am I allowed to know what exactly we are dealing with?"

"A *platzgeist.*" His pronunciation was solidly American.

"Huh. That's not a German word I recognize," Wilson said. He liked to think he had high fluency in German.

"That's because a German-speaking Texan coined the term in the 1920s," Morris informed him. "You familiar with zeitgeist?"

"Spirit of an age," Wilson replied as he paid for parking and pulled into airport traffic.

"Exactly, so it follows that a platzgeist is the spirit of a place, except there isn't anything romantic or poetic about it. If it's allowed to grow, we're going to have a lot of dead people. That's part of the reason we protect ghosts from being put in items—they help prevent a platzgeist from forming."

"This seems like something I should have known about," Wilson said drily, thinking about how close he'd gotten to the shadowy figure earlier today.

Morris heard the slightest hint of accusation in his partner's tone. "There's a good reason why you haven't. Sometime in the 1970s, we finally figured out how to combat them and prevent them from forming in the first place. The decision was made to keep quiet lest it become weaponized by the wrong people."

"We?" Wilson inquired. His mind returned to the fact that Morris was present at the founding of the treaty with the Minnesota State Fair ghosts and wondered if he was personally present for that decision as well.

Morris raised his forefinger and moved it back and forth between them. "The Mine. Us."

"But Haughton didn't know what it was either," Wilson objected. *How could the ghosts prevent platzgeists if they couldn't recognize one for what it was?*

"How's your grasp of the biology of ecosystems?" Morris switched to educator mode; he'd trained a lot of agents during his stint in the Mine.

Wilson was taken aback by the apparent non sequitur and the SUV that was just about to cut him off. He swerved and tapped the breaks before answering Morris's question. "I'm no scientist, but I read and watch nature shows."

Morris bobbed his head and started a little further back before continuing. "In a healthy diverse ecosystem, it's harder for an invasive species to take over because there is more competition for resources. For example, if you have a petri dish with one bacterial species in it, it's easy to introduce another and have it thrive. But it's a lot harder for that same bacteria to find an exploitable path to grow and reproduce if there are ten different species in the dish.

"That's what the ghosts are like for platzgeist. They don't have to actively do anything to prevent a platzgeist from forming. They just have to exist in that location. The more of them around, with all their different personalities, the harder it is for a platzgeist to develop to the point where it can manifest and do damage in our world."

Wilson put two and two together. "That's why we appease the ghosts. To keep them fat and healthy."

"One of the reasons. Ghosts are still the spirits of people and no one likes to go hungry." Morris's magic was rooted in empathy which he extended to those who were no longer living.

"Okay, so happy ghosts prevent platzgeists, but what

actually creates them?" Wilson inquired about their generative force. Morris was an expert on all things undead and Wilson wasn't one to waste such an opportunity to learn more. In a line of work where there were often more questions than answers, it was nice to have access to someone like Deacon.

"They are the fulmination of a singular emotional state, thus they tend to form where humans gather and experience a singular sensation en masse."

"Singular is doing a lot of heavy lifting there, Morris," Wilson wryly observed. "So the fair…?"

"Precisely. Fairs create a shared experience and a shared emotion."

"But surely, all the individuals at the fair are doing their own thing and experiencing different emotions," Wilson asserted.

"A fair as a whole creates a singular experience. Think about it…when someone says 'the state fair,' it elicits similar memories and associated feelings, regardless who you ask and which state fair they are thinking about."

"But the Minnesota State Fair only takes place two weeks out of the year. Is that enough time for a platzgeist to form?"

Morris answered rhetorically, "If the ghost population had been recently reduced and there's millions of people in attendance?"

"A perfect storm," Wilson answered his own question. He leaned back against the head rest. "But wouldn't that make that churches and sports arenas ideal for platzgeists?"

Morris shrugged his broad shoulders. "We don't really understand why, but holy places are immune to platzgeist activity. Sports arenas, on the other hand, have a shared experience but oppositional emotions: winning side, losing side. And we really don't have to worry about cities because there are a lot of ghosts there naturally and there are only a few times a year that they would have a singular experience—think New Year's Eve at Times Square. Most of the time, everyone is living different experiences albeit in close proximity to each other."

In light of this new information, Wilson made a decision. "There's something you should know about my encounter with the platzgeist that I didn't put in my report."

That got Morris's full attention. He shifted his weight to get a better look at Wilson. "Go on…"

Wilson kept his eyes on the road. "The physical description I gave was complete, but when I looked at the blinking lights, I had a sudden memory of my father and me walking down the midway at the Northern Idaho State Fair. After that, I think it *smiled* at me."

Morris gave it some thought before speaking. "I've never heard a platzgeist do that; it usually uses fear and scares people to death. But it is a creature with a connection to the land of the dead. Is your father dead?"

Wilson's face tightened and he swallowed hard before responding. "Don't know."

Morris recognized what he saw. "Bad memories?"

"Yes," Wilson said flatly. He intentionally avoided thinking about his past, much less talking about it, but he felt it prudent to tell Deacon.

Initially, it had crossed his mind that it could be the Smile in the Darkness, a powerful demon Wilson summoned when he needed crucial information of a certain caliber. During his last summoning, it had remembered his name, something Wilson had always taken great pains to prevent. He'd been on watch for signs of the demon ever since.

But the shadowy figure's smile didn't have any teeth. Smile always did. Still, it was good to know that the platzgeist used fear. There was plenty of that embedded in his childhood memories and he rather that than Smile on his trail.

Morris paused to respect the effort it must have taken the private man to reveal something from his past. It was the most Wilson had shared with him in all the times they had worked together. When he broke the silence, he spoke softly but deliberately. "I appreciate you telling me. Let me know if it happens again or something like it." Were it any other agent, he would have added "Be on alert" but he knew Wilson to be the most paranoid of the bunch. It wasn't like he'd teamed up with Hobgoblin….

The car was silent for a moment, and Wilson cleared the air by changing the subject. "If a platzgeist scares someone to death, why was Orhan frozen solid?"

"Platzgeists kill the living by forming a direct connection to the land of the dead. Most of the time, the connection is so terrifying that a person dies of a massive heart attack or stroke—not enough time for the cold to set in. For practitioners, they can fight off the fear with their will, but in the end, the unearthly cold gets them. The longer you fight, the harder you freeze. It sounds like Orhan put up one hell of a fight." Morris sighed at the memory of the first platzgeist victim he'd found frozen stiff.

"If he was trapping ghosts into items, he was a more than capable practitioner," Wilson concluded. "Even though I found the smoking gun—the *Expanded Daemonologie*—I didn't find the items. Everything powered by ghosts in the house was old. It's possible that he already sold them or stashed them somewhere else since he was killed *after* he knew someone was coming to speak with him."

"Could he be working with someone else?" Morris raised the possibility.

"If he was, I don't think it was a practitioner. I didn't pick up any other signatures at Orhan's house when I salted every room. Just his." Morris grinned; Wilson was nothing if not thorough. "I'm still waiting on the analysts for additional information: financials, storage units, real estate, safety deposit boxes. Until I know more, I was going to follow up on where he got his copy of *Expanded Daemonologie*—a local bookshop called Triangle Book & Binding."

Morris shook his head and chuckled, "Better you than me. Hunting down an entire print run can become rather Sisyphean."

Wilson shrugged in resignation. "I'm right there with you, but it's the lead I've got. I'm hoping one of the other copies leads to the items with the missing ghosts. Haughton fingered Orhan, but that doesn't mean he was the only one poaching."

"Work what your given, not what you want," Morris aphorized. "Reminds me of one time in Mayor's Income, Tennessee…" Wilson settled in for a good yarn for the rest of the drive. In his experience, Morris had an endless supply.

Chapter Eight

Falcon Heights, Minnesota, USA
28th of August, 9:26 p.m. (GMT-5)

Morris grinned when Wilson stopped in front of the horse trailer. "In here?" he said incredulously. The idea of Wilson being forced to muck in his expensive suit tickled his funny bone.

"I had to improvise," Wilson said defensively. "Needs must and all that."

Morris barked a deep laugh before getting down to business. "Fair enough." He pulled out the map of the fairgrounds that came with the parking pass and put his finger on Ag parking. "Tonight, I'm just going to get the lay of the land. We'll start here and walk this path." He moved his thick finger along the exterior streets.

"There shouldn't be any trouble, but be prepared in case the platzgeist does find us and try to attack. It's stronger at night and may be flush with new energy after its latest meal. Just keep a lid on it because we don't want to tip it off." He folded the map and slipped it into his pocket. "And no chit-chat. It only makes it harder to do my thing and I'm not getting any younger."

Wilson looked at him askance. *Because I'm the chatty one.* He summoned his will—*think, think, think*—and kept it wound tightly like a spring in his palm. "I'm ready."

Morris nodded and brought his will to bear. *I will fear no evil...* He collected the latent metaphysical energy and kneaded it, like a ball of dough. In his skilled hands, he started rolling it into multiple ropes that radiated from his person, then he sent them out.

Instead of breaking, they stretched until they were microscopically thin. They roamed everywhere, each acting independently like an octopus's many arms. They touched, prodded, and caressed everything in their wake. Even Wilson got the once-over, although it was so subtle that he wouldn't have known it if he hadn't been warned and just watched Morris perform the spell.

Morris tested his feelers, and when he received information back from the furthest of them, he nodded to Wilson. He was ready. Wilson followed close behind the husky man as he started along the path.

While Morris was very good at explaining things, words failed when it came to this spell. "You just reach out and feel the room. You know, pick up the vibe." But Wilson didn't know. No matter how many times he'd seen Deacon do it, he'd never been able to duplicate it, even when he academically understood the process and its affects.

Instead of sending out tendrils of his will, Morris was using his will to harness and use the existing metaphysical infrastructure. It was the difference between laying new cable and tapping into existing lines. It was harder to detect because it was a repurposing of what was already there, but it was temperamental work. Not enough power and the tendrils didn't communicate with the caster or they worked but didn't go very far. Too much power, and they burned out like an overloaded filament of an incandescent lightbulb. It was a whole other style of magic that eluded Wilson; simultaneously too delicate and too powerful for him to find the right balance.

Once they were out of the parking lot and into the fairgrounds proper, their pace slowed due to the press of the crowd, but that suited Morris's purpose. It allowed him to get more information from deeper in the fair while staying on its periphery.

They walked down lit streets, and the music from the kiddo rides twirled over the sound of other machinery and the ubiquitous white noise created by the throng of chattering humanity. The smell of food carts was a welcome change from the animal trailers.

It took Wilson back to those long summer nights of his youth. There wasn't much to do in northern Idaho, and the fair was a big deal. He understood what Morris meant about fairs being singular. Each had their own unique attractions and traditions, but they all shared in the same sense of communal spectacle. Variations on a theme. The smells and sounds nostalgically called to his internalized concept of the fair, even if it never happened that way in real life. He wasn't Minnesotan, but just walking along the outskirts of their state fair—which they called The Great Minnesota Get-Together—he almost felt like he might be. It was powerful stuff.

When they'd made a complete circuit, Morris released his will and the tendrils dissipated into nothing. He was breathing deeply and freely, like a runner who had just finished the race and no longer had to pace their breath. He removed his hat and daubed the sheen of sweat from his forehead with a handkerchief.

Wilson gave him a minute to recover before asking, "How is it?"

Morris shook his head. "It's bad. There are still ghosts, but not many. I have no way of knowing how many are in treaty with us without drawing the platzgeist's attention, but I suspect the lieutenant colonel is still with us. It's chasing something and I can see the ripples it caused in its wake, like watching a big fish swim after a little one in shallow muddy water."

"Greatest generation." Wilson added matter-of-factly.

"We got to give him as much cover as we can until we can fix this," Morris said as he put on his hat.

"Which means it's still fixable and you have a plan," Wilson extrapolated.

Morris smiled wide and his pearly white shone in the light.

"I've got a few ideas and some balls in the air, but before we go any further, I need some food. My stomach's been growling this whole time."

"How about a Pronto Pup?" Wilson suggested.

Morris shook his head. "I like my corndogs with corn. You ever had a Gizmo? A grilled loose meat sandwich of ground beef and Italian sausage served in a roll covered in red sauce and melted mozzarella. Put a little hot sauce on that and it's perfection." Wilson's mouth watered at the description.

Morris's grin turned mischievous. "It's been called a 'torpedo of pleasure.'"

"TMI, Deacon. TMI," Wilson replied as he followed him to a late dinner.

*****

It was late when they finally made it to Orhan's house. Wilson again parked down the block and they entered through the back door to avoid alerting nosy neighbors of their presence. The wards were already fading with their creator's death, so he didn't bother picking them, but he did slip his lock picks in the deadbolt he'd locked on his way out.

"Nice place, but not exactly your typical bachelor pad," Morris observed as Wilson switched on the lights. As far as the rest of the world was concerned, Orhan was still alive and flashlights in a dark house aroused much more suspicion than the idea that Orhan had stayed out late on a Friday night.

"I'm pretty sure it's inherited, but I'll know for sure when the financials comes in," Wilson replied. Intellectually, he knew it hadn't been long since he made the request, but the séance with Haughton felt like ages ago.

"Where's the body?" Morris inquired.

"Top of the stairs," Wilson answered. He pointed to the living room and motioned up and to the right. "You need me for anything?"

"No, I'm good," Morris replied and opened the black leather bag that held his particular tools of the trade. He pulled out a large silver cross, just in case. "Just stay down here. Shouldn't take long."

Morris followed the directions and climbed the stairs. He probed the body with his will before he carefully reached out with his fingers—still frozen, but no longer dangerous to the touch. He shaped a spell in his mind to get a bead on the platzgeist. *You shall know them by their fruits.*

As Morris was working upstairs, Wilson took a seat in the sitting room. The furniture was frilly but comfortable. He picked up the top book on the coffee table, a collection of works in the Barbizon school. He started flipping through like a bored patient in a waiting room. It was filled with realistic-looking paintings, all of which were unfamiliar to Wilson, who lacked both depth and breadth of artistic knowledge.

Art wasn't his thing, but he'd recently taken steps to

expose himself to it. He'd hoped learning about art would stoke his creative side and help his transmutation practice. He acknowledged the skill involved in creating lifelike paintings in a time before photography. He was beginning to be able to differentiate between major art movements and their associated artists. He could even recognize the famous works of big names. But his actual appreciation of art boiled down to "he knew what he liked." When he visited museums, he could see there was a big difference in seeing it live versus pictures in a book, but even when he found something he liked, he was done looking at it after a few minutes. He didn't viscerally understand people who could sit for hours in front of the same canvas to just *be* with the art.

He was plowing his way through the oversized book in his lap when he suddenly recognized a picture. It was a beige and white work of a young man and an older one working together to break stone. The image must have been a favorite, as the spine of the book was broken to this particular spread. He read the fine print in the lower corner: *The Stone Breakers* by Gustave Courbet, destroyed during WWII.

Neither the name of the work nor the artist rung a bell, but he knew he'd seen that painting before. Considering he'd never heard of the Barbizon school until five minutes ago, he was pretty sure it wasn't in another book. He racked his brain until it came to him—the basement stairs.

Wilson placed the book down and opened the basement

door to a framed *The Stone Breakers. Maybe it's a print?* he speculated as he took a closer look. Even in the poor light, he could see the paint was proud on the surface, showing all the textures of each individual angry brush stroke. He lifted the painting off the wall and brought it into the sitting room to compare it against the image in the book just to be sure. He might not know art, but he was a pro at Spot the Difference.

He mentally divided the image into sections and moved his eyes back and forth from the book to the painting but he couldn't find a discrepancy. He heard the floorboards shift under Morris's weight as he descended to the ground floor but kept his eyes fixed on the task at hand.

"What you got there?" Morris asked as he entered the sitting room.

"A painting hanging along the basement stairs. I thought it was an odd place to put a painting when I cleared the house, but then I found it in this book. It's supposed to have been destroyed during the war," Wilson explained himself.

The stocky man put his bag down and peered over Wilson's shoulder. He had a keener eye when it came to art and Wilson interpreted Morris's small noises and grunts as signs that he may have something. "It's good," he said simply.

"Good enough to be the original?" Wilson wondered.

"Good enough to ask an expert to take a look at it," Morris qualified. "Although this place is a little on the shabby side to house a priceless piece of art, if you know what I mean."

Wilson nodded; he'd visited the Moncrief family home. "Did you get what you needed upstairs?"

A grin pushed the fatigue from Morris's face. "I've got a good feel for it. Should make it easier to track it down and monitor it."

Wilson closed the book and put it back on the coffee table as he'd found it. "Then I'm going to grab the enchanted items from the curio and take this with us." He pointed to the painting. "Work won't miss Orhan until Monday, but that doesn't take his friends into account. Is he a still a popsicle?"

Morris nodded. "Yes, but thawing slowly. The cold from the land of the dead doesn't dissipate at normal speed. Did you get his phone?"

"Already cloned," Wilson affirmed as he went upstairs to collect the items. He took extra care to wrap the crystal figurines before placing them in the bag of salt.

Morris took a seat while he waited. He looked forward to a hot shower and soft bed at the swank hotel the Mine had booked for him, but for the time being, he was content to sit with the stone breakers and commiserate with them after a long day of work.

Chapter Nine

Minneapolis, Minnesota, USA
29th of August, 7:05 a.m. (GMT-5)

Wilson strode into the dining room for breakfast and found it mostly empty. They were staying at a high-end hotel downtown, the kind where guests pay for everything: internet, parking, phone calls, and the breakfast buffet. Business travelers had already come and gone, vacationers were still sleeping off last night's revelry, and anyone going to the fair could get a more reasonably priced breakfast there, which was saying something.

He immediately spotted Morris seated in front of a half-eaten plate. Instead of a suit, Morris was dressed in chinos, a polo shirt, and sneakers. Despite the casual wear, there was a hat on the table. Every gentleman should have a handkerchief and a hat.

Morris was on the phone but made eye contact and smiled to greet his partner. Wilson claimed the seat opposite him and made his way down the breakfast buffet. He loaded up his plate with a generous portion of home fries, scrambled eggs, and bacon while the bread toasted—if they are going to charge an arm and a leg, better get your money's worth, even if it was the Mine that was picking up the bill.

When he returned, Morris was wrapping up his call. "I assure you, Mr. Lopez, this is no joke. You get your crew together and I'll be there, with a bonus for the short notice." Morris nodded to reinforce the surety in his voice.

Wilson started eating and looked at the map of the fairgrounds spread out on the table between them. The folds and crinkles had been smoothed out and it was covered in different colored markings with arrows showing directionality. Solid dots peppered the map with times noted in military time next to them. To Wilson, a consummate student of military history, it resembled a battle plan.

"Looks like you've been busy," Wilson greeted him once he ended his call.

"Just lining my ducks in a row," Morris replied as he put away his phone and picked up his fork. "I worked it all out last night, but I'm going to have to spend the day at the fair to make sure it works on the ground."

"I'll give you a ride there," Wilson offered. "I have to drop off the ID badges to Jenkin at the Institute's booth before I stop at Triangle Book & Binding."

"I saw the incoming messages, but just scanned them. Anything interesting?"

"About six months ago, Orhan's aunt, one Patricia Miller, died and left him a sizable inheritance to the tune of several million in cash equivalents in addition to the house."

Morris whistled. "That's a lot of scratch."

"It gets better," Wilson added as he buttered his toast. "During their search, the analysts picked up a discrepancy between the statements of the Miller estate and Orhan's personal finances. Apparently, Ms. Miller had accounts and safety deposit boxes all over the state, as well as some out of the country. That prompted them to take a deeper look into Miller's history. Apparently she was investigated for art forgery twenty years ago, but no charges were brought due to a lack of evidence."

Morris tilted his head. "*The Stone Breakers* may be the tip of the iceberg."

"Exactly. I have an appointment with one of the FBI Art Crime specialists at the Minneapolis branch at noon. They were quite eager to take a look at something that might be the real painting." *That explains the boring suit*, Morris thought to himself; Wilson was conducting official business with a government agency.

"What about the bookstore?"

"Looks on the up and up. Long-running business registered with the state and none of the owners are in our system," he spoke obliquely even though there was no one else in the room. "According to their taxes, the binding side does a lot work with the university and the bookstore is more of a side enterprise. I checked their website last night and it looks very new age. They have a rare books reproduction line. *Daemonologie* was listed as out of stock and available by request only."

Morris pushed his empty plate away and folded up his well-marked map. "Looks like we each know what we have to do today. Meet you in the lobby in fifteen minutes?"

Wilson sipped his coffee. "Sounds like a plan."

*****

The fair opened every day at six in the morning, but the foot traffic before nine was still mostly exhibitors, vendors, and workers. Their pass got them into vendor parking and once they were past the gate, they parted ways. While Wilson strode purposefully to the convention hall, Morris strolled to his first destination.

The sky was dotted with clouds, and cool breezes blew through on what promised to be a warm day. He took a right on Judson Avenue and waved at the group of nine people dressed in semiformal attire. Six of them had hard cases: two violins, two violas, and two cellos. Three were clearly there as muscle, carrying chairs and music stands. "Good morning," Morris hollered as he closed the distance between them. "So glad you could make it. You all look perfect."

The older man holding a violin case stepped forward. "Mr. Moore?"

Morris smiled wide. "The very same. And you must be Mr.

Lopez." He reached into the side pocket of his medical bag and retrieved a white envelope containing fifteen hundred dollars. "As promised, half up front, half at the end of the day. It's okay, I won't be offended if you count it."

The other violinist took Lopez's case as the older man verified the amount. He tucked it into the inner pocket of his jacket. "I have to say this is the strangest offer we've gotten in a long time." Heads bobbed behind him in agreement.

"I'm just another patron of the arts," Morris did his best to allay their suspicion. "Did you get my email about the route and the pieces?"

Lopez hesitated. "I did, but we couldn't get our hands on the kazoos. None of us own one and it's not something the Minneapolis Orchestra keeps on standby." The sextet was supposed to end each performance with a kazoo rendition of the first twenty-three bars of Beethoven's 5th.

Morris noted that the man had waited to mention that until *after* taking the money. "No problem," he answered. "I brought some for just such a contingency." He reached into his bag and produced a clear plastic sack containing six brand-new kazoos still in their brightly colored boxes. "Hold onto these for tomorrow, and remember, no explanations. Let the music speak for itself."

Lopez looked back at his companions, giving them one last chance to ask questions or object, but they stayed quiet. "All right, let's set up. We've got a performance in fifteen minutes."

He distributed the kazoos as the crew set up the chairs in an arc and the musicians extracted the instruments from their cases.

With the musicians set, Morris checked his watch and the map. "I have to go, but I'll be coming by periodically. Just stick to the schedule and we'll settle up for today at the last stop."

"We'll be where we're supposed to be. Have no doubt about that," Lopez attested. Well-paying side gigs were always welcomed, and he wasn't asking them to do anything illegal or unsavory. It helped that the pieces were relatively easy and everyone loved the fair.

The sounds of their warm up and tuning faded as Morris headed north to the Butterfly House. This group was significantly younger, dressed in cargo shorts, t-shirts, tank tops, and cut-offs. "Are you the University of Minnesota Go Club?" Morris asked as he approached them.

A serious-looking Asian man in his late teens or early twenties stepped forward. "Mr. Moore?"

Morris nodded. "There aren't many of you," he commented on the handful of people present.

"More are coming, but some of them didn't get the message until this morning. Everyone I've heard from is in," he insisted.

"That doesn't affect how much *we* get paid, right?" a young woman with pink and purple stripes in her blonde hair asked.

"Everyone that participates and follows the schedule will get paid," he reassured her. "But because ya'll are here on time, you get half up front. The rest will have to wait to get paid at the end, and I'll be stopping by throughout the day to see who shows up when," he said sternly.

Being students, they came at a cheaper rate than a sextet culled from the Minneapolis Orchestra. They might have even done it for the free tickets plus food and beer money, but the promise of a hundred dollars a day to play Go at the fair was too sweet of a deal to pass up. Morris handed each of them a fifty-dollar bill, which some stared at like it was some sort of foreign currency. He fought the urge to tease them about how this was how people paid for things back when phones had actual dials.

They pulled everything they needed to play from their backpacks and satchels: a bowl of white stones, a bowl of black stones, and a rolled up canvas Go board for each pair. Four of them started games while the fifth watched the time and waited for others to trickle in. They were supposed to play at specified spots at particular times for a fixed amount of time, but otherwise, the day was theirs. Morris marveled at their ease at copping a squat—*Ah, to be young again.*

He next took his creaky bones westward to the West End Market. The troupe from Guthrie Theater in downtown Minneapolis was milling about, intrigued to meet their mysterious benefactor. When they were first approached to perform at the fair, they'd hoped it was a last-minute fill at the Schilling Amphitheater, but as the details rolled in, it was clearly something else.

"Good morning, ladies and gentlemen!" Morris greeted them like a circus barker. "Isn't it a wondering day to perform al fresco?" he asked rhetorically.

A tall brunette with striking cheekbones stepped forward and extended her hand. "You must be Cedric Moore. I'm Charlie Fields. We spoke on the phone earlier?"

Morris shook her hand; her grip was firm and direct, like her demeanor. "Nice to meet you. I'm so glad you were able to find enough actors on such short notice."

Fields smirked. "The theater has a shortage of patrons, not actors." In exchange for a per diem and a hefty donation to the theater for new costumes and scenery, they were tasked to act out small tragic scenes from various plays in their repertoire at different spots on the fairgrounds. There was some speculation that it was a hoax until a sizable wire transfer hit their account—a down payment to let them know the offer was legitimate.

They kept the props to a minimum because they would be on the move, and the first performance was scheduled in front of the animals in the exercise yard just to the south. Shakespeare in the Park? More like Shakespeare in the Stockyard. But as they say in the theater, the show must go on.

"I'm thrilled at this opportunity to bring theater to the public. No tickets, no seating, no lofty stage; no division between the actors and the audience," Moore laid it on thick before handing over an unmarked envelope to the director.

"For expenses." Fields peeked inside and ran her thumb across the edge of the brick of bills.

Satisfied, she secured the money in a pouch under her clothing and against her skin. "Will you be staying for the performances?"

"I won't be able to see all of them, but I can stay for the first one," Morris agreed. This was the last of the three groups he'd employed for the day and he wouldn't need to make the rounds for another hour or so. It seemed as good as any place to see if he got his math right. Plus, there was sparkle in her eye that warranted a closer follow-up.

Chapter Ten

Benjamin Frye carefully tied off the last backing stitch, and the short, pudgy man held the book block up to the light to examine it from all angles. He smiled at his work, deepening the crow's feet on his round face. He'd earned every fine line and wrinkle honestly with a lifetime of grinning that infectious smile of his. Time may not have been kind to his hair or waistline, but his smile hadn't lost its warmth or radiance.

He wiped his hands on a rag pulled from one of the many pockets of his worn overalls. He placed the book block into the backing machine and closed the vice upon it. With the sewn pages held in place, he could fix the individual sections together to prevent shifting under use. He reached for a backing hammer and began beating the spine edge over its neighbor, starting from the center and working his way out. When the rough work was done, he finished it with a large metal roller, evening out any irregularities from the hammer. He ran his finger along the spine and found it as smooth to the touch as expected. *Anything worth doing was worth doing right.*

It was a far cry from the first books he made as a child: folded ruled paper with construction paper covers saddle-stitched with his dad's chunky old Swingline stapler. Once upon a time, he'd tried to fill his little books with his thoughts but he never got further than a few pages. He got much more satisfaction from making them than writing in them. When he was a young man, he considered it a deficit he should overcome, but he'd long since made his peace with his temperament. Some people lived in a world of words; he was happy making his books.

When the master bookbinder who'd trained him decided to retire, she offered Frye the option to purchase her workshop. He wasn't born a man of means, but he scraped together what he could and they worked out a plan of transfer between them. He not only inherited the location and equipment, but more importantly, the existing clientele.

The business from the University of Minnesota's library system was reliable, and after several years of massaging the relationship, it now paid all his bills, leaving him free to pursue other ventures that were less steady but more profitable, like the one that had drawn him to the workshop on a sunny Saturday.

The adjacent bookstore had come later, after he met the love of his life. Cyril Nowak was a serious erudite man, the perfect yin to Frye's yang. After a few dates, Frye suddenly found words worth putting in a book while Nowak was at a loss of them for the first time in his life. Nowak was a successful civil engineer who'd spent years living overseas, moving from one project to another, and when the empty property next to Frye's workshop came up for sale, they decided to purchase it.

Nowak had figured it would be a piece of cake. He'd built skyscrapers, hotels, arenas, and billion-dollar complexes; surely, he could turn an abandoned retail space into a workshop and bookstore that offered custom bookbinding. Some people say planning a wedding is the ultimate test of a relationship, but clearly those couples hadn't renovated together. After knocking out the non-load-bearing interior wall, rearranging the layout, and completely redecorating, Triangle Book & Binding was born and the Solomonic triangle—a circle inscribed in an equilateral triangle—had become an icon in the Minneapolis new age and spirituality scene.

Everything was good for Frye and Nowak until they'd taken an LGBT cruise and met Alejandro Garza. That's when everything turned great. They'd never thought of having a third member in their relationship, but they'd both fallen for the younger man and he for them. Within the year, they were all living and working together in communal bliss. Frye loved the new irony of the store's name—although Nowak was quick to remind him that it was coincidence, not irony—and the fact that their friends now referred to them as the ABCs.

While Frye and Nowak's belief in the unseen was rooted in blind faith, Garza knew it to be real. He'd always been able to see things and know things that he shouldn't have been able to, and gently, oh so gently, he'd introduced them to the world of magic. The adjustment took some time and new boundaries had to be drawn, but with Garza's help and premonitions, their new family thrived.

"Ben," Garza called from the front of the store. "You know how I said I had a bad feeling when I woke up this morning?"

Garza made it a habit of informing his partners of his emotional state every morning at breakfast. They knew his abilities were real, but how he felt didn't always correlate to what eventually happened during the day. When Nowak had started keeping records—data was the foundation of good judgment—it confirmed what Frye suspected and Garza knew: Garza was more right than wrong. When he had a bad feeling, everyone took precautions. It was like when the weather forecast called for rain; even though the meteorologist didn't always get it right, you still carried an umbrella.

"Yes," Frye answered without lifting his head from his work, measuring the book block against the eighth-of-an-inch-thick birch plank he'd selected for the boards. He liked to use real wood for his high-end reproductions and followed the old adage: measure twice, cut once.

Garza walked to the back to put more space between him and the front door. The bookstore was supposed to open at ten and he normally opened a few minutes early, but he'd left the door locked and the sign display to "closed." He spoke from the threshold. "It's getting worse. I think *something's* coming."

It was the fear in his voice that got Frye's attention. Garza was dramatic and demonstrative, occasionally to the point of hyperbole, but rarely afraid. He'd had a rough childhood and knew how to handle himself in the face of frightening things. If something rattled Garza, Frye knew it was serious.

Frye immediately stopped what he was doing and looked up at his partner. "I'll get the gun."

He went to the safe and pulled out the Ruger Super Blackhawk he'd purchased with the workshop. The neighborhood used to be a lot rougher than it was now and thankfully, he'd never had cause to fire it in self-defense. Even after gentrification had really taken hold several years ago, he'd kept it clean and licensed, just in case. It was a monster of a pistol. He hoped that the sheer size of it would be enough to scare anything away but loaded it with bullets all the same.

Frye stepped in front, Blackhawk held low and pointed away and to the ground. Garza followed close behind. The interior lights were still dimmed, making it easy for them to spot the small man dressed in a suit standing outside the locked door. "Oh my God, Ben, he's so bright!" Garza exclaimed, looking away at the bright aura. He'd always been able to see magic and those who could practice it, but he'd never seen anything like this. "Be careful!"

They watched him check his wristwatch before pulling out his phone. Within seconds, the phone at the counter rang. "Should I answer it?" Garza whispered.

"No, let's see if he goes away," Frye said quietly. In that

moment, he made a decision. *If he tries to break in, I'm firing.*

Wilson hung up after the fifth ring triggered the prerecorded message with their location and hours. There were no signs indicating they were out of town or some emergency had preventing them from opening, but if no one was there, it made breaking in a viable alternative. There were no wards on the door and the electronic security was a joke. He shielded his eyes from the glaring reflection of the sunlight and peered through the window. He saw two figures standing behind the counter and he knocked on the glass to get their attention.

They jumped at the sound and Wilson exaggeratedly pointed at his watch. "We can't very well pretend we didn't see him now," Garza muttered as he smiled and waved. "I'm going to let him in but keep the gun ready." The muscular man kept his shoulders back, head high, and stride strong. The only hint of his fear was the unconscious clenching and unclenching of his chiseled jaw as he flipped on the light switch and walked to the front door with the keys.

Wilson stepped back as Garza flipped the sign to "open" and unlocked the door. Garza was halfway back to the Frye by the time Wilson entered. "Good morning," he bid the two men.

"Morning," Garza replied stiffly, keeping his gaze off Wilson. His eyes were slowly adjusting but it was still hard to look at him straight on. If they managed to get out of this alive, he just knew he was going to get a migraine.

"Are the owners in?" Wilson inquired.

"You're looking at two of them," Garza responded with a hand gesture that indicated Frye was the other half. "If you are looking for Cyril, he won't be in until after lunch."

"That's enough to constitute a quorum," Wilson joked, but neither of the owners laughed.

Frye leaned on the counter, keeping the gun out of sight. "Is there something we can do for you?"

"I'm looking for the King James *Daemonologie*," Wilson said. "I heard that you're making custom copies."

Frye relaxed a little. "I've got a backorder on one of them right now. The soonest I could get a wooden-boarded version to you would be about three, maybe four weeks. They're expensive," he warned.

"Sold a lot of them, huh?" Wilson fished for information.

"A handful. They take a while to make," Frye answered vaguely. It was music to Wilson's ears, much better than learning there were hundreds of them.

"The reproductions are remarkably well made, but what I'm really interested in is the original. How much would it take for me to buy that from you?"

Neither of the men had expected such a request. "Sorry, but it's not for sale," Frye said firmly. Wilson summoned his will for a little magical persuasion. *Think, think, think…* Garza saw the ball of motion whirl in Wilson's aura.

"He's about to cast!" Garza yelled to Frye.

The older man whipped the Blackhawk out from under the counter. "None of that, magician!"

The warning told Wilson a few things: both knew about the existence of magic, and the tall Latino was sensitive to it, although he was probably not a caster or the shop would have been warded. He immediate stopped casting and raised his hands slowly to convey nonaggressive intent, but he kept his eye on Frye's trigger finger. The second it moved, he would spring into augmented action.

"Easy fellas. I'm willing to compensate you fairly for the book. I'll even cover some of the lost income from its reproductions. I'm not an unreasonable man but that book is dangerous."

"We don't sell anything dangerous," Frye rebutted truthfully. They'd decided early on to not do any business with magical books because they thought there were too many risks involved. In fact, they avoided magic in general, and most of the few objects they had were things that Garza had acquired prior to their meeting.

Wilson didn't mince words, even with a gun pointed at him. "Then you have a hard time telling what's dangerous. This book has resulted in the death of one person and put many more lives in jeopardy. Ask your partner if he thinks I might have more insight on dangerous magic than him."

"But it's not magical," Garza objected emphatically. Wilson read the burst of emotion as guilt—he didn't like the idea of being responsible for something bad happening.

"Just because a book isn't enchanted doesn't mean what's inside isn't dangerous. Knowledge can be the most dangerous thing in the wrong hands, or applied in the wrong way," Wilson countered and tried a different tactic. "You guys seem genuinely surprised about the *Daemonologie,* but if you don't help me prevent it from getting out, more deaths will happen again and those calamities *will* be on you."

"Who the hell are you?" Frye asked without moving his gun.

"Who I am is unimportant. However, who I work for isn't," Wilson answered with deliberate obfuscation that conveyed a very important threat: he wasn't a single person, but part of an organization. Their problem wasn't going to go away just by getting rid of him.

"And what organization is that?"

"A group of like-minded magicians tasked with keeping harmful magic out of the hands of ordinary people," Wilson fibbed.

"And you're willing to pay?" Frye asked.

"Yes, and I'll also need the name and addresses of the other copies you've sold. They all have to be accounted for before anyone else dies. But more than that, I'd really love to no longer be on the business end of a .44," Wilson added. Frye hadn't taken his finger off the trigger the whole time.

Frye exchanged glances with Garza who gave him a nod. Wilson hadn't moved a metaphysical muscle since he'd raised the alarm, and Garza was quite certain that if the mysterious man had wanted to kill them, he would have done it by now and quite easily. Frye lowered his weapon but didn't put it away.

"Thank you," Wilson said sincerely. "I'm going to lower my hands and reach into my jacket now. It's to pull out money to show you I'm acting in good faith." He slowly extracted an plain envelop filled with hundreds and handed it to Garza.

"He's serious," Garza told Frye after he'd finished counting it and checked the bills to make sure they were real.

"So what's your name," Frye asked.

"Dee," Wilson replied. When he didn't want to use any of his aliases, he fell back on the first letter of his name. He didn't need this bouncing back on his Institute of Tradition or Discretion Minerals aliases and he certainly wasn't going to give him his real name.

"Oh, like the movie," Garza said knowingly.

"Pardon?" Wilson feigned ignorance.

"You know. 'This is the last suit you'll ever wear.' Or… 'Best of the best of the best, sir! With honors!'" He acted out the lines.

"Oh no," Wilson laughed it off. "That's just a coincidence. Plus, mine's blue."

Garza looked past the blinding aura and finally noticed the fine cut of his suit. It was conservative and boring, but as he said, it was blue, not black.

Frye made a decision and went with it. "Why don't you

come into the back, Mr. Dee? That's where I keep the original." Frye suggested. "Alejandro, could you gather the information for the ones we've already sold?"

Garza nodded and logged into the computer that functioned as their point-of-sale register. As he started compiling the names, Frye and Wilson made their way into the workshop.

It smelled like leather, oil, ink, and paper—like a library and automotive shop weirdly rolled into one. It was a place where things were made. Wilson stood back, giving Frye some privacy to open the safe. He exchanged the Ruger for a beaten and battered book. What was left of the leather binding was crumbling and pilling, and Frye gently placed it on a nearby conservator's lectern. "There is it, the original."

Wilson opened it up and, although showing the appropriate spotting, the pages within were in remarkably good condition given the exterior. "Why haven't you rebound it?"

"This has been rebound several times already." Frye pointed to the extremely narrow interior gutter. "To rebind it, I'd need to add paper to every page, and that would be a lot of unnecessary work, especially as it serves its purpose as is."

"How do you mean?"

"Look around, Mr. Dee. I'm a bookbinder, not a printer. I use this to make a true copy of the interiors," Frye explained as he pulled a small black pen nib from one of his pockets.

"This is a Perry & Co. N°1417 dip pen nib, manufactured in 1873. If you attach it to a freshly plucked chicken feather and provide it the appropriate supplies—paper, ink, blotter, sand—it will make an exact duplicate of any text you set next to it."

"Ah," Wilson uttered, suddenly understanding why Orhan's copy had been such a good facsimile. "May I?" Frye nodded and expected Wilson to take it in hand, but instead he just stared at it intently. "How exactly does it work? Does the nib ever produce a copy from something that is no longer in proximity?"

Frye shook his head. "No. It doesn't have a memory as such, and it can't do illustrations or decoration. I print the decorative pages I need on the screw press, assemble the rest of the book with the right number of blank pages, and then set it next to the 1417. By the morning, I have a copy."

Wilson nodded. "I didn't sense anything malevolent about it, but you should know that all magic comes at a cost. If you feel comfortable using it for your business, that's fine with my organization as long as you don't use it to reproduce dangerous works."

"We thought we were safe as long as we stayed away from magical books," Frye said, dumbfounded. "How do I know if a non-magical one is dangerous?"

"If you have an old book that isn't magical and the subject material has nothing to do with magic, spells, demons, or devils, you're probably fine, but if you have questions, here's a number you can call." Wilson handed him a business card with just the Salt Mine's hotline number printed on it. "Leave a message with your name, number, and the work you're curious about and someone will get back to you." Frye slipped the card into his pocket with the nib.

Wilson got down to business. "Now, what would you consider reasonable compensation for the original?"

Frye tilted his head. Nowak usually handled the accounting, but he wasn't going to drag this out any longer than necessary. "How about we make it equivalent to selling five reproductions in addition to the original. $4,000?"

"Done." Wilson held out his hand and the two men shook over it.

Frye closed the *Daemonologie* and delivered it to Wilson like it was a dirty diaper. "Someone really died because of this?" he asked with a mix of incredulity and remorse.

"Indirectly, yes," Wilson replied, tucking the wrapped book under one arm and pulling out his wallet. "The person didn't know they were in danger, so they didn't take the proper precautions." He handed Frye the difference from what was in the envelope he'd already given Garza.

"It looked normal to me. What was so dangerous about it?"

"I'd rather not say. Just knowing would bring you more headaches," Wilson sidestepped the question.

Frye heard the register's printer whirling as it warmed up. "It sounds like Alejandro has the customer list ready."

The two returned to the counter just as the printer spat out a single page. Frye reviewed and confirmed its contents against his memory before handing it to Wilson.

"That's all the people that ordered them," Garza said, "but the last one doesn't actually have the book. He ordered it online last week but Ben hasn't gotten around to making it yet and he's not going to be able to now." He must have overheard some of their conversation in the back as he continued, "We'll have to notify him and refund his money. And remove the book from the website. And check our entire inventory for anything that could also be questionable. And—"

Frye interrupted and stopped him before he could spin out. "We'll take care of it, Alejandro."

The page was still warm when Wilson got his hands on it. He scanned the names: six copies, all but one local and he already had Orhan's copy. The out-of-town order had gone to Taiwan. That one was out of his immediate reach; something for an Iron Mine agent to handle. Wilson folded and tucked the paper into the inner pocket of his suit. "Thanks for your cooperation, gentlemen. If you encounter something questionable or outright evil, or a magician that is not as reasonable as me, you can call that number I gave you. We'll take care of it…it's what we do."

"What number?" Garza grilled his partner; he'd missed that part of the conversation.

Frye pulled out the business card and handed it to him. "To contact his organization." Garza flipped it around and handed it back to Frye once he saw there was nothing written on the back.

"You guys have a lovely store. Five stars, customer service is thorough but intense…" Wilson spouted a theoretical review on his way out. The men nervously chuckled as the door shut behind the enigmatic Mr. Dee.

Frye put his arm around Garza. "You did good."

Garza let his partner support him as he let his brave facade drop. "The one morning I agree to open for Cyril…" he muttered under his breath.

Chapter Eleven

Falcon Heights, Minnesota, USA
29th of August, 11:05 a.m. (GMT-5)

The pleasant weather drove up opening weekend attendance; warm and sunny was always a welcome respite from the long and harsh Minnesota winters. Newscasters were out in force, repeating some variant of "If it keeps up, we're in for a record-breaking day here at The Great Minnesota Get-Together!" Regardless of where the smiling reporters framed their shot, there were always children goofing off in the background and distracted elderly visitors oblivious to the cameras.

Morris took off his hat and fanned himself with it. The sun had burned away the clouds and the coolness of the morning had passed. In conjunction with the humidity from all the nearby lakes, it started to remind him of his native Louisiana but with more white people and whole lot more dairy.

He sipped his fresh lemonade and considered his next move. So far, the three groups he'd employed were sticking to their schedule, all part of an organized effort to disrupt the collective fair experience and the subsequent energy that fed the platzgeist. His idea was simple: drain the emotional energy during the day and be gone by night. Give it no quarter and give it no contest.

He believed he could take the platzgeist now, but it was an exercise in futility without the ghosts to prevent it from reforming, especially since the fair had just started. If necessary, he could keep this up until Labor Day—the final day of the fair and the unofficial last day of summer—but he didn't relish the idea of beating the pavement day after day. The sooner Wilson found the items containing the ghosts, the sooner he could put the platzgeist to bed permanently.

But his strategy wasn't just to reduce the total energy. He also wanted to change the emotional geography of the fair, damming it in some places and redirecting it along different paths in others, thus the meticulous planning of locations and times. As the bard once wrote, there was method in his madness.

Its purpose was three-fold. First, he needed to give Lieutenant Colonel Haughton some cover and starving the platzgeist was a good start. Second, it made it easier for Morris to detect where the platzgeist was—fewer metaphorical streams and rivers to lose the scent. Last, he was preparing for an inevitable confrontation in what he still referred to as "spiritual warfare," even if he wouldn't use such a term around his fellow agents. By slicing off whole sections and bottlenecking others, he was reducing supply lines and cutting off paths of retreat.

The fair was huge, and he had many more circuits to go

before that time could come. He took a seat at one of the ever-present benches to rest his feet before the next bout. He tipped his hat at the elderly couple juggling their corndogs and drinks on the next bench over. He pegged them somewhere in their 80s, and they ate in that comfortable silence cultivated over a lifetime together—one of those couples who had said everything so many times over, it didn't bear repeating.

The man politely nodded and the woman smiled. "Nice to have a seat, isn't it?" Her voice warbled with her age.

Morris returned her smile. "Yes, yes it is."

"First time here?" she asked curiously.

"Oh no, I've been here several times before but it's been a while," he responded affably. Morris was used to complete strangers striking up conversation. He had that effect on people.

"I've been coming to the fair every year for seventy-four years!" she proudly exclaimed.

He widened his eyes to affect surprise. "Well isn't that something! That's dedication. You should tell one of those newscasters about it. They're sure to put you on TV."

Her eyes twinkled mischievously. "That's for next year's visit. Always have to have something to look forward to at my age."

"Hazel, would you let that man be? He didn't come here to jaw with some stranger," her husband said. His tone was gentle, making the words less harsh than they could have been.

"It's no bother," Morris interjected. "I've got nothing

pressing, and I always have time for a pretty lady on a sunny day."

The older man rescinded his objection under his wife's raised eyebrow. It was her way of saying, "See? There are people who still have good manners."

"I bet the fair has changed a lot in your time," Morris set her up to share her experiences. That's what she really wanted: a reason to converse and have someone to listen to her stories that hadn't already heard them a thousand times. He didn't mind being her soundboard, and he paced his lemonade consumption to run out right around the time he needed to start his next circuit.

She talked about showing animals as a girl and her ribbon-winning pig in the junior division. How she loved riding the carousel and had taken her own kids to the same one—not the new one in front of the grandstand, but the real one that used to be in the midway—and how she was in the stands at the air show crash. They hadn't had any air shows since and she missed them. The new airplanes they used now—she'd been to other air shows—were too modern and didn't have the same sense of style the old ones did anyway. She'd even met Larry, her husband, while she was working at the All You Can Drink Milk Stand.

By then, even Larry got sucked into the conversation and chuckled. "You were the prettiest thing in that silly costume they made you wear. She had her hair in double braids—looked like the girl on the old Swiss Miss boxes."

Hazel blushed. "And you had all your hair and teeth. We were both younger then."

Morris shook his head. "Youth is wasted on the young."

"You got that right," Larry agreed.

Morris knew the time but made a show of checking his watch. "I'm due to meet someone but it's been a pleasure. Hazel, Larry, you two have a blessed day."

They waved Morris off as he headed south to make sure the University of Minnesota Go Club hit their mark. The crowd had picked up and he found himself in the same position he'd been so many times before: surrounded by the ignorant flowing masses of humanity while striving to protect them from the consequences of their own hubris. His was a lonely road, which made the Hazels of the world shine all the brighter. They were small, personal reminders that even though there may be a rotten ones in the bunch, people were still worth saving.

He arrived at the Turkey To Go stand and found the college kids where they were supposed to be. Their numbers had tripled since this morning and they had five games going. Those that weren't playing were stuffing their faces with Buffalo turkey wings except for the one who was eating a salad from God-knows-where. Morris hadn't seen anything that wasn't fried or breaded or covered in sauce since he'd arrived. He waved, letting them know he was checking up on them again and those who weren't playing or reeling from the spicy sauce waved back.

Next were the musicians, and he heard them long before he could see them. They were playing the last bars of Ludwig Spohr's "String Sextet in C major, Op. 140" when he found himself on the edge of the gathered crowd. The spectators clapped as they finished and the musicians put their instruments down. The audience murmured with amusement when the kazoos came out. The sextet took their cue from the head violinist and began humming Beethoven's 5th with vigor. Once everyone recognized the piece, there was a roil of laughter and more than one captured the performance with their phone.

Morris had applied his will sparingly throughout the morning but took the temperature of the area with a thin metaphysical tendril. He could feel the ambient power of the fair diminish, just as it had among the early morning crowd that had watched the death scene of Romeo and Juliet performed passionately in front of a pen of indifferent horses. With each pass of the different groups, the channels would get narrower and narrower, depriving the platzgeist of energy. He dissipated his will and after the sextet collectively took a bow, he caught their attention and gave them broad smile and courteous nod.

He'd saved the best for last and approached the theater troupe as they were breaking for lunch, which Morris had staggered on his master schedule. Fields smiled when she saw him and gestured "just one minute." He waved at the tall brunette and took a seat, waiting patiently for his lunch date.

Chapter Twelve

Saint Paul, Minnesota, USA
29th of August, 11:50 p.m. (GMT-5)

The Warren E. Burger Federal Building was like so many other institutional buildings built in the 1960s: an unimaginative and unadorned rectangle of concrete and marble. It reflected the ethos of that time, one that valued function over artistry while simultaneously projecting power, like the fascist architecture of the early twentieth century but with even fewer frills. This particular expression of cold and soulless modern architecture would later be called Brutalism—minimalist constructions with plenty of exposed concrete, a predominantly monochrome color palette, and little to no ornamentation or structural elements. To Wilson, it was just another government building. It didn't need to be pretty to serve its purpose.

Upon entry, he ran headlong into security. They were curious about his Glock and the large rectangular object wrapped up in the blanket but gave him passage when he provided his CIA credentials and appointment time with FBI Art Crime. His steps echoed in the spacious lobby as he walked to the building map to find his destination. The FBI only claimed a portion of the building; the majority functioned as a US district court.

Normally, Wilson would have taken the stairs, but *The Stone Breakers* was just large enough to be difficult to carry. As he waited for the elevator, he wondered how many similar buildings he'd been in and what it was about bureaucracy that created such forgettable banality. By the time he reached his floor, he concluded that imagination and individuality was antithetical to systems of power and considered the mystery solved.

The hallways were pretty barren, but there was always someone working through lunch, even on a Saturday. He took a few turns and checked in with the receptionist manning the front. He carefully set the painting down before taking a seat in the waiting area.

He pulled out his phone and checked his messages. He'd sent the Mine the list of *Daemonologie* buyers to check for practitioners and found none except for Orhan. He would still use caution in retrieving their copies, but there were plenty of non-magic users that were into the occult and old books.

"Mr. Wilson?" the receptionist called his name. He looked up from his phone. "Special Agent Rowland-Smith is ready for you. If you'll follow me." Wilson put away his mobile and grabbed the unwieldy painting by the frame. He was led to an interior room labeled CF6. *Unmemorable and unimaginative*, he noted to corroborate his earlier observation.

The door opened to a windowless room with two long tables and an array of lamps to provide better lighting than the fluorescent strips in the ceiling. "Here, let me get that for you," a feminine voice offered once the door opened.

Special Agent Rowland-Smith was a sturdy woman dressed in a fitted suit with a fashionable brooch pinned to the collar. Her auburn hair was pulled back in a knot and her top-rimmed glasses gave her a scholarly look. She took the painting in hand and manipulated it out of the blanket and onto the table with the grace of one who'd done the same thing many times before—careful but sure. She gazed upon *The Stone Breakers* for a brief moment before turning her brown eyes to Wilson. "Mr. Wilson, I presume? I'm Special Agent Rowland-Smith of FBI Art Crime."

Wilson shook her hand. "Thanks for seeing me on such short notice."

"We always make time for our compatriot spooks," she said dryly, "especially when something of such interest comes up." She went to the other table where various pieces of equipment had already been laid out. "Have you worked with our division before?"

"No, but I'm always interested in learning more," he replied.

She bobbed her head to the side as she gathered the materials she needed and put them in sequential order next to the painting. "Without taking this to a permanent lab, I'll only be able to perform a cursory examination, but there is quite a lot we can learn using some simple tools and a lot of applied knowledge. It will be about twenty minutes, give or take."

Wilson nodded and let Rowland-Smith get to work. She set *The Stone Breakers* on an easel and switched on a bright light. He silently watched her move and change the angle of the light multiple times, just looking at it. He could only imagine what her trained eye could see that his could not.

She jiggled the mouse and woke up the computer she'd set up in anticipation of his visit. Plugged into the USB port was a wand with a light of its own at the end. "This is an optical microscope…well, the travel version," she said out loud for his benefit. "It helps me take a closer look at the surface of the work."

As she passed a wand over different sections, she turned her eyes to the blown-up image on the screen. Wilson marveled at how much more detail was visible. He could see streaks of different colors loaded on the same brush, and the peaks and troughs of individual strokes. Watching the monitor, the composition as a whole temporarily lost its cohesion as she zoomed into its constituent parts, like standing too close to one of the giant Monet's.

Occasionally, she made little noises or muttered under her breath. He wasn't sure if she was talking to herself or the painting, but he stayed quiet, lest he interrupt the conversation she was having in her head. Everyone had their process. Eventually she put down the wand and grabbed a can of compressed air, gently removing the light surface dirt with short puffs at distant oblique angle.

"We're going to go dark," she warned him before switching off the lights. She turned on a flashlight and *The Stone Breakers* lit up under the ultraviolet spectrum.

"A black light?" he speculated.

"UV light. It covers a wider spectrum than a black light," she replied. A yellow-green haze floated over the entire work from the varnish, but the paint underneath shone through in wildly different colors. The whites glowed bright yellow and the bits of red a dark pink.

"All paints and varnishes develop fluorophores over time, which glow under UV light. The older it is, the brighter it shines. If we know a piece has been repaired or restored at some time in its history, we would expect to see discrepancies in luminescence at that location. It's part of using the known history of a painting to establish authenticity," she spoke in generalities.

She put on a pair of goggles and switched flashlights. Wilson deduced it was infrared when the room went pitch black.

"And what's infrared for?"

"It lets me see what's under the darkened varnish and paint. It's often used to hunt down signatures, and it shows the pattern of craquelure without the distraction of the actual colors," she answered, passing the beam over the breadth of the canvas. "All old paintings have cracks so we're looking for the right pattern. In this case, perpendicular to the radiating lines of stress originating in the corners. It's not an infrared reflectometer, but it's good enough for a first pass."

She took the goggles off when she was finished and turned the overhead lights back on. "This is a lovely piece. Whoever did it was extremely competent. It checks all the boxes for a painting done in 1849 on preliminary examination and the temperament of the work could easily be Courbet's."

"But it isn't the real one," Wilson read between the lines. "Could it be a forgery?"

Rowland-Smith burst out laughing and waved her hand in front of her face. "Oh dear Lord, no! *The Stone Breakers* is 2.57 meters long and 1.65 meters tall. Whoever made this copy kept the same proportions, but this is *definitely* not an attempted forgery."

Wilson blushed. "Oh."

"It that doesn't change the fact that the artist, whoever it is, has a remarkable talent of mimicking the work of a renowned painter. Next time, I would recommend that the CIA check the dimensions *before* calling on the FBI Art Crime Division."

"Of course. My apologies for wasting your time," Wilson regained his footing.

"Don't worry about it," she graciously replied with a smug smile. "It was worth it just for the story, and viewing beautiful works of art is never a waste."

Chapter Thirteen

Minneapolis, Minnesota, USA
29th of August, 12:52 p.m. (GMT-5)

Wilson returned to his hotel room with his hands full: the reproduction of *The Stone Breakers* under one arm, the *Expanded Daemonologie* under the other, and a to-go sack with lunch. He hoped food would improve his mood—Martinez had accused him of having a case of the hangries on more than one occasion—but even after he ate, he was still peeved. It had been a long time since he'd been so professionally embarrassed, even if it wasn't his fault—the analysts should have done their job.

He stowed the original *Daemonologie* with Orhan's copy and pulled out the customer list. He had three copies to track down but now it seemed tangential to the case at hand. He needed to find the fair ghosts Orhan had trapped, and the fishy financials looked more promising. The dead end with *The Stone Breakers* didn't change the fact that Miller's estate and Orhan's finances were incongruous.

He pulled out his phone for another look at what the analysts had sent him. Even though Miller died months ago, her estate had only recently closed, transferring all her various bank accounts and safety deposit boxes to Orhan. If Orhan wanted to hide the items, he had his pick of hiding places.

Wilson ran through the list, looking for a place to start. His task wasn't made easier by the fact that Orhan hadn't yet consolidated or closed anything. The analysts gave the box number, bank location, and opening date of each safety deposit box that was now under Orhan's name. He paused his scroll when he found one that was opened recently: two days *after* Orhan found his aunt dead in the basement.

His mood brightened at the prospect of a lead. Orhan had gone forty-odd years without needing a safety deposit box. What did he suddenly need to keep safe and out of his aunt's estate records?

Wilson looked the bank up on his phone and grabbed the keys to the rental car. It was a local branch with truncated Saturday hours, and if he missed this window of opportunity, it would be closed until Monday morning. He didn't have time to go to Orhan's house to hunt for the box keys, which meant he would have to improvise.

Riverland Bank was a small regional operation and the branch in question was inside a renovated warehouse called the Fisk Building, which had been turned into an interior mall of sorts. It was a clever way of repurposing a large old brick warehouse and Wilson couldn't help but note the architectural similarities between it and his beloved 500.

With twenty minutes to spare, he took the time to memorize the appearance of a Minnesota driver's license and Orhan's information and signature. If he was going to fake them with magic, it would be a lot easier if he had a clear imagine of them in his mind. Then, he gathered his will and entered.

It was a large branch with multiple tellers and cubicles separated by frosted glass dividers for those that needed to see a banker. He hovered away from the tellers and he didn't have to wait long before a pockmarked, sandy blond man in an ill-fitting dress shirt and slacks approached him. He looked more like a surfer than a banker as he introduced himself as Bill. Bill had worked at the bank long enough to know the risks of something complicated walking in through the door right before closing and was relieved when all Wilson wanted was to access his safety deposit box.

Wilson was immediately taken down to the basement where Riverland had installed a refurbished Diebold 1871 bank vault that held all the safety deposit boxes. He visually swept the confined area and immediately identified the cameras. He reached into his pocket and hit the electronic disrupter on his saltcaster, killing the cameras in and around the vault. It was unlikely that anyone was monitoring them in real time, but good tradecraft was a reason unto itself. Should they have cause to review them in the future, the absence of footage might arouse suspicion but it wouldn't fall back on him specifically.

"Box number 8291," Wilson informed Bill, who unlocked

the cabinet that held the signature cards.

"Mr. Orhan, I'll just need your photo ID and John Hancock," Bill answered with a cheesy grin.

Wilson presented Damon Warwick's photo ID and coated the plastic with his will. It made the Michigan driver's license appear Minnesotan with a name, address, and signature matching Orhan's. When it came to visual glamour, it was much easier to coax the mind to see what you wanted when there was a physical prop that fit the bill.

Bill checked the name and signature on the ID and even checked to make sure the picture matched the man before turning the sign-in log toward Wilson. "Just sign and date on this line," he instructed. Wilson signed using another glamour that would disappear as soon as the book was closed.

Wilson gathered his will as Bill fished out a large keyring and found the correct key. "This way into the vault." When Bill turned to ask Wilson for his key, Wilson released his will, sending the bank attendant into a temporary catatonic state. He stood in place, gently swaying with his mouth open and face blank.

He grabbed the key from Bill's deadened hand and engaged it in the first lock. He then pulled out his lock picks and got to work on the second. Wilson turned his back to the vault entrance in case there were any passersby so they wouldn't be able to see what he was doing. He could just as easily be having trouble with the key. After all, a bank employee was standing right there.

The actual lock posed little challenge. Like many safety deposit boxes, it wasn't that difficult to pick. They relied upon the distributed two-key system and the physical location within a vault for the majority of their security. The problems he'd encountered with them came from old locks that hadn't been taken care of or from those that didn't work properly due to shifting of the vault's foundation over time.

Under his ministrations, the small rectangular door popped open and he checked it for magical wards before sliding out the long box from the wall. Inside, he found a bunch of papers, a leatherbound book, and several pieces of jewelry. He peeked through the hag stone to see if anything was magical, and the jewelry lit up against the dull mundane world.

He didn't have time to investigate further; his catatonia spell was effective but short-lived, and he wanted everything put away before Bill came to. He removed the papers and book and dumped the jewelry directly inside his Korchmar Monroe attaché without touching it. He placed the book and paperwork on top and eased the empty metal box back into the wall before relocking the door. He returned the key ring to Bill's mindless hand and guided him back to the desk where he'd confirmed Wilson's identity.

Then, Wilson waited for the magic to wear off. As soon as the glaze fell from Bill's eyes, the blond squinted at the migraine that was coming on, an unfortunate side effect of that particular spell.

"Sorry to hear you're not feeling well, Bill," Wilson said sympathetically, as if they were engaged in a sociable exchange. "Thanks for your help. Have a good weekend and see you next week."

Bill nodded, but it hurt to move his head and he elected to wave instead. It took him a second to get his bearings but once he recognized where he was, his brain filled in the missing bits. He started putting everything away, starting with the log book. The signature and date looked in order, and he closed it before returning it to the cabinet along with the bank's box keys and the signature card.

Wilson turned off his electronic jammer as he walked upstairs and exited the building. He drove half a mile and pulled into a residential neighborhood to look at what he'd found. He carefully removed the papers and journal and ran his will over the enchanted items, but none of them contained ghosts. *Damn it,* he cursed.

He scanned over the paperwork as he put it back in his briefcase. There were a lot of financial papers, deeds, and a stack of Minneapolis municipal bearer bonds issued in the late 1970s—at least $200,000 worth. Then he found a handwritten note:

My dearest Stringbean,

If you're reading this, I'm no longer on this mortal coil and you've done what I asked you to do even though it sounded a little crazy to you at the time. There was so much that I couldn't share with you to justify my strange request, but suffice to say I am not who you thought I was. Or rather, I'm not -only- who you thought I was.

For decades I forged fine art, and that is how I really built my fortune. I would have told you sooner, but my silence was a form of protection against my former associates—the fences and dealers who peddled my creations and the people and institutions that purchased them. But now that I'm gone, you need to know the truth to protect yourself; be wary of anyone who approaches you and tells you they are an old friend of mine. I've compiled files on each of them, as much as I know, and you can use that to make sure they stay away.

I hope you don't think too badly of me. It's a hard pill to swallow as an artist, knowing your creative work will only amount to copies of dead painters' masterpieces, but I made my peace. And I won't lie, it was awfully fun to fool the experts.

However, I haven't just gifted you my profits and perils. I have also left you a recipe, something I tinkered with over the years and finally perfected. I'm inordinately pleased that I figured it out and I couldn't rest if I never told anyone about it, even if it's posthumously. None of the others would understand. They aren't special like you and I.

You'll have to suss out the steps in my journal, but I think you're clever enough to put it together. Maybe you'll even follow in your aunt's footsteps? If you do decide to pick up where I left off, be careful. It's one thing to rip off rich pricks who have to have a painting at a price that they know is suspicious, and another to rip off those capable of siccing a demon on your ass.

Regardless, it's in your hands now. Choose wisely and live well.

From beyond the walls of death,

Aunt Patti

Chapter Fourteen

Minneapolis, Minnesota, USA
29th of August, 3:27 p.m. (GMT-5)

It had taken some time for Wilson to spread out the paperwork on the floor of his hotel room and grasp the scope of what he had: the details of a twenty-year-long art forgery ring. He had titles of paintings, sale locations and dates, buyer names, types of transactions, and revenue distribution. Some of the biggest auction houses and art institutions were implicated in the documents. He worked with a gleam in his eye, collating and processing them for the Mine.

Ultimately, Leader would decide what to do with the information but he put in a request after he'd sent off the final picture: if it *was* turned over to the FBI Art Crime Division, he would like it to be given to Special Agent Rowland-Smith with Wilson's name attached. *Worth the story alone. Indeed…*

With that finished, he systematically stacked the papers in order before putting them away. It was time for the main event: Aunt Patti's journal. He cracked his knuckles and released the elastic band on the moleskin journal. Upon opening, he found all the pages had been deliberately separated from the spine.

How odd, Wilson thought to himself as he flipped through. They were still in order—each was numbered on the bottom right, many with capital letters by them.

On first glance, it was a diary with some but not all of the entries dated. It was written in mixed mediums—sometimes ink, other times pencil—and every so often, there was a sketch of hands to the side. Wilson didn't draw, but he knew that hands were notoriously difficult to get right and a common exercise among artists. He used to tease Alex that his sketches of hands looked like they belonged to a Simpsons character.

The ink color changed from entry to entry and some of the writings in pencil were done with art pencils, not standard No. 2s. From that, Wilson surmised that Miller kept the journal with her while she worked and wrote with whatever she had nearest at hand.

Reading other people's diaries was tedious at the best of times. It was filled with things people knew better than to say out loud but felt and were compelled to share nonetheless. He started at the beginning and found it disjointed. The subject matter jumped around so much with long digressions about people and personal subjects that he wondered about Patricia Miller's state of mind in her later years until he stumbled upon a delicious idea: it was a forgery of a journal. The note to Orhan wasn't from a senile aunt, after all; its author was sharp with a sense of humor.

Wilson approached the journal from a different angle: the

book was in code and the fact that the pages were loose was significant to breaking it. He went page by page and separated them into piles by medium, putting all the sections written in red ink in one stack, then the blues, etc. Then, he re-read each stack in chronological order. They made more sense but were still far from coherent. There was a second sequence of the code he was missing, perhaps even a third.

Appetite whetted by a good old-fashioned code break, he considered the author and the intended audience. It had to be something that both would know well, something that they had in common or talked about. It couldn't be anything too random or Orhan would never be able to figure it out. Perhaps a book cipher or a substitution or transposition cipher?

He played around with the pages and the journal case itself, looking for clues. He reviewed sections several times and his eyes strained to read the yellow ink in the soft sallow light of the hotel room lamps. *Have I ever seen yellow ink before?* The thought floated by. Obviously it existed; there was probably a whole rainbow of colors out there for artistic ink pens, but he'd never seen one in an office store.

His mind latched onto a single word in his internal monologue, waiting for his conscious thought to catch up. *Rainbow.* ROYGBIV: red, orange, yellow, green, blue, indigo, and violet. He checked his hunch by flipping through the blue stack and found two distinct shades of blue ink. Had he been more artistically inclined, he would have initially separated blue from other blue instead of lumping them together in one pile.

He checked his phone to see which one was blue and which was indigo and put the stacks in order. When they still didn't make sense, he tried reverse order: VIBGYOR. "I need another step," he sighed as he took a step back. His stomach growled. "And some more food."

He ordered room service—grilled cheese, tomato soup— and kept plugging away, this time focusing on the entries written in pencil. Gray wasn't in the rainbow mnemonic. Where did it fit in Miller's code? Wilson turned to the internet and got a crash course on gray. Turns out, it wasn't even on the color scale, just a continuum between white and black.

He broke for an early dinner when the food arrived. Maybe he was taking it too literally? What if the words on the page don't actually mean anything, even to Orhan? He ran with the idea and spread out each page on the floor by color and looked at them en masse.

The hands. Miller was an accomplished artist and master forger—she didn't need to practice drawing hands. All of hers were already quite realistic. So why so many hands? He started counting the number of fingers showing on each picture and found they increased as he moved up the rainbow, but there were gaps. He spliced in the gray sections to complete the ordinal count and finally got the message Miller had intended for Orhan's eyes only, spelled out in the capital letters beside the page numbers: BE SURE TO DRINK YOUR OVALTINE.

"You've got to be kidding me!" Wilson exclaimed in a mixture of pride and frustration. He'd solved the puzzle but the victory felt like a rip off. *Was all this an elaborate joke?*

Wilson forced himself to relax and look at the facts dispassionately. He'd found the papers put back in sequential order in the moleskin, which meant either Orhan didn't even try to figure it out or he wanted to hide the message his aunt had left him. That would imply the message was something important, something worth protecting. A person who had just been pranked wouldn't have taken the time and effort to reset the prank. He'd only do that if it wasn't a prank.

A Christmas Story was an American classic from the '80s, a nostalgic look at growing up the '50s that had quite a bit of satire and social commentary for the adults, but all the emotional highs and lows of Christmastime that every kid could relate to. He recognized Miller's message as the same lousy Ovaltine advertisement the main character had slaved over, but it had been so long since he'd seen it. He pulled up the clip to see if there was something significant in the scene in light of what he knew about Miller and Orhan. As he watched, he felt more than a little sympathy for poor Ralphie, but otherwise came up short. He read a synopsis online to see if it sparked any inspiration, but as far as he could tell, the Ovaltine reference was just another bit from an iconic movie, like "fra-gil-e," the leg lamp, and the pink bunny suit.

Wilson sulked as he put the pages back in order, breaking his own supposition that the pranked wouldn't do so, and wrapped the elastic band around the journal to make sure the pages stayed put. He placed the journal together with the other papers and set them next to the bagged magical items he'd taken from Orhan's house. The lump of the Syco-Slate made it difficult to arrange neatly, but he managed after fiddling a bit. *What a strange thing to make magical*, he thought again absentmindedly. The other items he'd confiscated were all traditional, but that one was an oddity.

He was about to close his luggage when he stopped, remembering what he'd seen at Orhan's house. His interest in the curio case was in finding the magical items, but there had been a shelf of old bottles and cans as well, a slice of Americana: Coca-Cola, Folger's, Campbell's, Burma-Shave, Quaker Oats, Spam…and an orange and white can of Ovaltine with a pry top lid!

His original plan was to wait until dark to return *The Stone Breakers*, but he couldn't wait that long. He had to see if there was anything inside that can. He grabbed the painting and his keys and drove to Orhan's. He let himself in the back and returned the painting to the basement stairs. He took one last look at it before switching off the lights; Special Agent Rowland-Smith was right. It was a lovely piece.

Wilson climbed the stairs and checked Orhan as he passed the landing: still cold and stiff but no longer frozen to the carpet, with the slightest give on the extremities. In another day or two, he'll be fully thawed, just in time for him to be missed at work.

He entered the bedroom and everything looked the same as yesterday. He opened the curio case and extracted the can of Ovaltine from the vintage display. With his keys, he pried the lid open and found a folded stack of pages inside along with another handwritten note from Miller. *I knew you'd figure it out! Be careful, Stringbean.*

Wilson skimmed the stack of printed material. He wasn't the technician that Weber was, nor was he the theoretician that Chloe and Dot were, but he was magically educated enough to understand what he held and his heart dropped in his chest as he read. It was instructions for forging magical items.

Chapter Fifteen

Whenever a practitioner made a magical item, it held the esoteric characteristics of its creator. It was why they had magical signatures on salt casting: the imprinted will of the magician was still trapped inside the object. Even if they were powered by ghosts, the maker left its mark.

Beyond the imprint of the essence of their will, the maker also left signs of their craft that a forger would have to get right: the mundane equivalent of using the materials and techniques appropriate to the time and place it was created. That's what Miller had figured out: how to make an enchanted item look like it had been made by another magician.

Wilson's mild reeled with the possibilities and his first instinct was to go back to his hotel room and salt all the items he had. It was a task that got pushed to the bottom of the list once Wilson had found no ghosts or only old ghosts in the items. They were, de facto, of no material importance to the case and would get salted as part of their intake processing at the Mine and given to Chloe and Dot for a full assessment that

Wilson couldn't hope of equaling on his best day.

But now, immediate salt casting was called for. Would Miller's technique fool the saltcasters? Would he even be able to tell? It was still light out when he arrived back at the hotel, and he sent Deacon a message to stop by his room when got back from the fair. There was too much to explain in a text.

Once inside, Wilson carefully removed the enchanted items recovered from the curio out of their storage bags and laid them out a foot apart from each other on the short carpet. He grabbed his saltcaster and blew three rounds in quick succession. The salt danced and a signature formed in front of each object. There was a variety of signatures—two belonging to Orhan, four with the same unknown signature, and the rest a mixed bag—but what captured Wilson's attention were the six items with solid white disks of salt.

The only time he'd seen that after salt casting was when someone had the potential to become a practitioner but hadn't developed as a magician. However, anyone making a magical item would have performed enough magic to have a distinct magical signature. It was a paradox. He snapped pictures to document his find and sent it to Chloe and Dot.

Next, he removed the five magical items he'd found in the safety deposit box and salt cast them. Two of them had the same signature as the four curio items, one had a unique signature, and two of them were blanks. *Why were these in the safety deposit box? What was so special about them?* He took pictures of all of

144

them, not just the blanks, and sent them to Chloe and Dot with an URGENT tag.

He considered the items with blank signatures. Except for the Syco-Slate, they were all pieces of jewelry, which was to be expected when it came to enchanted items, especially the older ones. They were portable, could be worn without arousing suspicion, and because they had mundane value there was less risk of being discarded over the years. From the curio, there was a pin decorated with jade, two plain gold rings, solitaire diamond earrings, and a pair of sapphire earrings. The pieces from the safety deposit box were two gold necklaces. They had different link patterns and one had a small enameled blue and white Russian Orthodox cross on it.

His phone dinged with a message from Deacon: he was leaving the fair and on his way. The screen abruptly changed as his phone rang. Wilson looked at his phone incredulously. The caller ID said Dot was calling. Dot *never* called.

"This is Wilson," he answered.

She skipped over the pleasantries. "Where did you find the silver ring with the cloudy amber and the necklace with the cross?" The road noise in the background explained why Dot was doing the talking—Chloe was driving. Dot hated driving so much that even though she was on the left side and Chloe on the right, they had imported a van from the UK and had it customized to accommodate their unique anatomy.

"A safety deposit box in Minneapolis."

She laughed sharply. "Of course. It's always something like that."

"What are they?" Wilson asked curiously.

"They *look* like the ring and necklace of Rasputin."

It took a second for that to sink in. "Do we have his signature on file?" One of the advantages of salt casting was being able to capture the signatures of deceased practitioners via the items they had enchanted during their lives.

"Of course," she replied and Wilson could hear her roll her eyes at him. "But I'm not in the Mine right now. We'll be there in about…" her voiced faded away and he heard snippets of an exchange between her and Chloe. "…in about an hour. If it were up to me, it would be sooner, but you know, dead weight."

Wilson grunted an affirmative even though he found it odd. If Dot had seen Rasputin's signature before, she should be able to identify it—she had an eidetic memory. However, his primary rule when working with the twins was to always support Dot whenever Chloe couldn't see or hear him. The second rule was do the same in reverse. "Let me know when you know."

"You know, if *someone* would just pull over and look at the phone, we could settle it right away," Dot laid the sarcasm on thick, even for her. Wilson heard "okay, fine!" in the background and Dot's voice perked up. "I'm pulling you on speaker."

He heard Chloe's voice pipe in over the passing cars. "Hi

Wilson, give me a second to look at the pictures you sent."

He awkwardly waited on the line and Dot wasn't one to fill the silence with social chitchat. "Well, what do you think?" Dot impatiently prodded her sister.

"Yes, that is Rasputin's signature on the amber ring," Chloe confirmed, "and the necklace *looks* right, but what's with the blank signature?"

"I'm not sure, but I found a note from a practitioner that claims to have figured out how to fake the provenance of enchanted items," Wilson mixed jargon to get his meaning across succinctly.

"What?! That's impossible," Dot objected.

Like that's ever stopped the impossible from happening, Wilson said to himself. "I'll get you the items and the paperwork and you can be the judge."

"Sounds good," Chloe chimed in. "We have to go. Good luck on the case."

"And don't you dare lose that ring!" Dot menaced. He was about to respond but the sudden silence from the other side of the line let him know she'd already hung up.

Wilson put the phone down and brought the ring and two necklaces to the writing table for a closer look. He gathered his will and started with the ring.

Every practitioner left cultural traits in how they wielded magic indicative of where and when they lived, how they were trained to practice, or a mix of both if they were incongruent.

It was like language. Everyone spoke with an accent and vernacular, and there were often differences within the speakers of the same language, even when they are mutually intelligible. It was one way to tell where someone was from or where they had learned the language if they weren't a native speaker.

For example, Wilson could self-identify his work as being whitebread American—as opposed to Martinez's work, which was still American but with a definite Latina influence—or how he could peg Hobgoblin's work as Modern European with a Germanic tinge.

He ran his will over the ring and it screamed Russian, metaphysically speaking, which made sense. It was hard to get more Russian than Rasputin. He noted the maker's marks that he encountered and quickly retreated. Wilson had a healthy mistrust of magic rings in general, and the fact that it was Rasputin's made him even more cautious. Most of the time, demonstrative people claiming to be magicians were phonies. But when they were the real thing, it often meant they weren't firing on all cylinders and he preferred to avoid interacting with those magicians, even if only via their creations.

Next, he examined the necklace with the Orthodox cross. The knots of will had all the features that Wilson associated with Russian work: strong and massive internal structure ornamented with delicate filigree in all the right places. The decorative scrolls ran the same orientation as the ring's.

The fact that it wasn't powered by ghosts was par for the

course. Traditional Russian methods forewent using ghosts as power sources and instead relied upon the caster's own personal strength, which always struck Wilson as odd, considering how long serfdom had persisted in the Russian Empire. He didn't find anything he didn't expect to see, which was exactly what a forgery was supposed to do.

He picked up the plain gold necklace and gave it the same treatment. Were he not so knowledgeable about Russian magic, he might have been tempted to call it Russian, but it wasn't. This was more akin to an American speaking English in a Russian accent. It was a "moose and squirrel" of forgeries. It would only be capable of fooling those that didn't know Russian.

Wilson withdrew his will and moved the chain back and forth over his hand. *This was a practice sketch*, he judged. *A piece of trial and error to work out the kinks.* "Holy shit! You did it, Patti," he said to the empty room.

The firm knock on the door grabbed his attention. "Who is it?" Wilson asked before opening the door.

"It's Moore," the resonant voice rumbled from the other side. "You wanted to see me?"

Wilson opened the door and Morris looked beat, hat and paper bag in hand. "Come in, I've got something to show you."

"Can we do this sitting down?" Morris asked as Wilson closed the door behind him. "My dogs are barking." He came to a dead stop when he saw all the salt-casted items spread out on the floor. "You've been busy. Any of these got the fair ghosts?"

Morris dropped himself onto the sofa and Wilson took the chair beside it. "No, but I've stumbled upon something bigger."

That got the older agent's attention. Wilson wasn't prone to exaggerate and he sounded honestly excited. "Okay, shoot."

"Dear old Aunt Patti was a seasoned art forger, but she didn't stop with paintings. Somehow, she acquired the ring of Rasputin and used it as a guide to forge the necklace of Rasputin."

"So the painting *was* a forgery?" Morris asked.

"No, but I gave Art Crimes a good laugh when I asked. Apparently, the original is huge, like almost nine feet huge," Wilson said dismissively as he retrieved the ring and necklace from the desk. "Take a look for yourself. Chloe confirmed the ring's signature is Rasputin's and the necklace has all the right metaphysical detail to pass as a necklace made by Rasputin. If it wasn't for the solid disk on salting, I wouldn't have been able to tell it wasn't authentic."

Morris didn't take the statement lightly. Wilson's beef with the Ivory Tower—in particular with Alexander Petrovich Lukin—was well known. He'd interacted with them more than the other agents, and he'd dedicated a significant chunk of his studies to understanding the ways of his enemy.

"And Orhan knew about this? The magic forgery, not the salt casting," he clarified as he examined the pieces for himself.

"I think so. I found the instructions hidden in his bedroom and there are handwritten notes on them that don't match Miller's cursive," Wilson explained his thinking.

Morris pointed to the other items with solid white disks still on the floor. "So what's the story with those?"

"Not sure. They contain ghosts but they are all old. Maybe Orhan was studying his aunt's work?" Wilson wagered a guess.

"Think that's what Orhan was up to, trying to use ghosts to power a forgery?"

"Maybe," Wilson hedged before running with the idea. "And if he was, maybe he got spooked when he found out I was coming into town and stashed the evidence of his misdeeds in one of the many safety deposit boxes he has around the city. I only had time to visit one today but I can hit it hard on Monday."

Morris rose to get a better look at the items. "The jewelry, I get, but this is a little left field," he said as he squatted down and picked up the Syco-Slate.

"Miller had a sense of humor. What's more ironic than a vintage divination toy actually being enchanted by a trapped ghost?" Wilson asked rhetorically.

"You went to the bookstore right? Was it Miller or Orhan that bought the copy of the *Expanded Daemonologie?*"

"Orhan bought it four months ago."

"So unless Aunt Patti also happened to know how to trap ghosts, Orhan must have made this or bought it," Morris reasoned. He examined the Syco-Slate and found it smooth to his will, but it seemed somehow *off*. He heightened his gaze and poured his full attention to the surface and found that under the smooth exterior, it was rough, like lacquer applied over coarse sandpaper. "Did all these items come from the curio?" he asked Wilson, pointing to the other five items with solid white disks in front of them.

"Yeah," Wilson answered with the sinking feeling that he'd missed something. Morris silently picked up the pin next, then the diamonds, then the sapphires, and last the rings. He broke into laughter. Wilson sat up in his chair. "What is it?"

"*These* are the items we're looking for, hidden in plain sight," Morris said when he finally recovered.

Wilson picked up the Syco-Slate and focused his will on it. "But it's smooth."

"Only superficially. Think about it. People tea-stain fabrics to make them look older than they really are. Furniture restorers scuff up and match the stain on a repair so the new wood looks original to the piece. So, if you were trying to make a new magical item powered by ghosts look old, what would you do?"

"You'd find a way to coat it to hide the roughness," Wilson answered before collapsing back into the chair with a look of defeat. "It makes sense. Orhan's aunt warned him that ripping off magicians was dangerous. The kind of people buying Rasputin's necklace might send a demon after you for ripping them off, but people buying a nondescript pair of enchanted gold rings? He found a way to use her knowledge without attracting the potential ire of the more-powerful among us."

Morris handed him the paper bag he'd brought from the fair. "Don't beat yourself up too badly. On first pass, it felt smooth to me as well. I suspect I'm simply more attuned because of the work I mostly do."

Great, I'm the flashlight and Deacon is the infrared reflectometer, Wilson grumbled to himself. "That may be, but it happened on my watch. My responsibility, my fault." He opened the sack and found a short stack of chocolate chip cookies.

"Except the moment I got called in, it was no longer just your responsibility. I could have checked the items, but I didn't. That's not on you," Morris pointed out.

Wilson paused. "You're right. You really bungled this one, Deacon."

The reply was so unexpected that Morris had to look up to see if Wilson was serious or joking. The subtle hint of a shit grin on Wilson's normally-stoic face answered his question. He'd heard he'd changed since his disappearance and return last year, but Morris hadn't expected jocular ribbing *and* a rejoinder.

The older man shook his head. "I'm trying to make you feel better. Shut up and eat your cookies."

Wilson complied, even though he wasn't one for sweets. He took a bite and mmm'ed. "Damn, these are good."

Morris took the bag and pulled out a cookie for himself.

"You should have had them when they were still warm."

Wilson was mostly done feeling sorry for himself by the time he ate the last gooey bite. "So we have the items. What do we do now?"

Morris leaned back and helped himself to another cookie. "Tonight, we rest up. Tomorrow, I put down the platzgeist and release the ghosts."

Chapter Sixteen

Falcon Heights, Minnesota, USA
30th of August, 2:49 a.m. (GMT-5)

Like many creatures, it didn't remember its beginning, only that it suddenly was—infinite darkness in a still and barren womb, indistinguishable from all that surrounded it. For so long, there had been nothing else except it.

Then the slimmest slit of light appeared in the endless plane of blackness. In the searing beam, it saw it was separate. It was it, and everything around it was not-it.

It went to the light but the crack was too narrow for it to pass. It was the first sign that there was more than cold darkness and hunger, and it clawed and ranted and railed against the opening, but it efforts were futile against the immutable sliver. It lapped up the light and survived on its scraps, but the more it ate, the more hunger gnawed at it.

Time passed, but it didn't know time. It didn't pay any attention to it because it was not-it. If it had, it would have found that it and time were not so dissimilar. Time was also indifferent to everything that wasn't it. Instead, it came to understand that it was alone and trapped.

Slowly, the crack grew larger and like the light, it grew stronger until it was able to pry the gap open at a glacial pace. On the other side, it discovered warmth. It was bathed in so much light, all that it could eat, and for the first time it wasn't hungry.

But it drew the attention of the creatures of the realm. They hated it and hunted it and forced it back into its hole. They repaired the breach and shut it into darkness. It was once again at the place of its origin, only this time, it knew of things other than nothingness and longed for more.

Like time, it kept worrying at the seams—jawing, clawing, slavering, and raving at it. It had forgotten the emptiness that wasn't it. It had even forgotten that it was hungry. All it wanted was to get back into the warmth, to bask in the light. Eventually, the rift opened again and it slipped through once more.

This time, it was ready for the cruel luminous creatures. The prey had become the hunter and it absorbed their light before they could warn the others. Before they could gather a posse and chase it back into its hole.

At first, the light it consumed had burned, and it lay on the ground and thrashed as strange memories flooded into it. It was no longer alone. The not-it was now part of it, and the more creatures of light it consumed, the more it knew. It had a name, platzgeist, the realm of light was called the land of the dead, and more importantly, it learned there was an even brighter place beyond the land of the dead, if only it could find a way in.

*****

Wilson groggily woke from a dreamless sleep and found his way to the restroom. Half-awake in the middle of night, his hotel room blurred into the platonic form of all the ones that had come before: bed, nightstand, lamp, and the light from the hallway dimly illuminating his path to the toilet.

The cold bathroom tile on his bare feet roused him a little. As he relieved himself, he wondered just how many hotel rooms he had stayed in, but he shut his brain off before it started to do the math. That was a surefire way to sabotage going back to sleep, and he needed his rest. He'd felt off this whole mission and he wanted to wake fully refreshed and fully himself.

He returned to bed, burrowed under the covers, and closed his eyes. He grabbed one of the pillows and rolled onto his side, appreciating the heavy weight of the blankets. When he traveled, he always turned the thermostat to chilly. He found the sense of being bundled and holding something in his arms comforting.

Northern Idaho was cold as hell during the dead of winter and the trailer had done little to keep the chill out. It was made worse because his father had covered the heating vent in his room with one of his surplus military crates "to teach the sissy to be tough." Wilson had spent the winters buried in blankets and holding Max, their German Shepherd, for warmth. He could still smell that old dog.

He dug in deeper and tried to clear his mind, but the memories persisted, demanding his attention—the time his father had forced him to steal and drag six old wooden shipping pallets from the loading docks at the pipe factory to fix the porch for the trailer. How he'd made him disassemble them using only basic tools and laughed when Wilson jumped back in fear every time his father slammed the hammer down an inch away from his raw hands. How he always smelled: cigarettes, Cutty Sark, and disdain.

He remembered lying in bed praying that this time Max would stop his father from beating him. Stop the shadow that lingered outside his bedroom. It would sway back and forth, moving the light beneath the door in a silent alarm as his father worked himself up into a frothing anger at the worthless kid his bitch of a wife had had. Probably wasn't even his, and he could already tell he was some kinda boy-lover. He wasn't going to have no boy-lover kid.

But Max never did. He remembered how sad Max's eyes had been while he was being beaten. How it seemed as if he was trying to tell the boy something—tell him the trick to not getting beaten, tell him how to properly submit to the bigger animal, how to soothe it with something other than bruises, blood, and broken bones.

That once ever-present creeping fear came back, starting

at the base of his skull and moving all the way down. Wilson opened his eyes, reassuring himself that he wasn't there anymore. All of that was over. Done. History. No different than any of the other things he'd read about that had happened in the past.

In the relative dark of the hotel room, the ambient light flickered. Out of the corner of his eye, he caught a shadow swaying back and forth in the hallway outside his door.

Without thinking, he was out of bed and on his feet. An explosive rage detonated in the lower parts of his brain and fed an incandescent cascade of will. Metaphysical tendrils wrapped around him, enveloping him in electric armor, and he slammed his will against the hotel room door.

It crumpled before him, hinges torn from the metal frame. It flew across the hallway and he heard it crash against the far wall, but his eyes were fixed on the black shadow standing at the threshold. The door had been the only thing that had spared it the full wrath of Wilson's will, and it immediately winked out of sight.

The remains of the door shook Wilson out of his primal state. It was plastered to the wall on the other side of the corridor and looked like a cannon ball had hit it. His higher executive cognitive functions kicked in and he immediately calculated the next course of action. First, he picked up his mobile and called in for air support.

"What?" Morris gruffly answered on the fourth ring.

"The platzgeist was here," Wilson said flatly. "I made a

mess."

Morris awoke in an instant. "I'll be right there," he responded crisply.

Wilson then went to the hotel phone and dialed the front desk. "Someone just broke into my room! 515. Please hurry!" He slammed the phone down to sell it and grabbed his luggage. Everything for the mission was already inside, and he quickly packed his clothing and toiletries. He gave himself less than five minutes before management and security would show, but hotel guests on the floor could be out in the hall any minute.

He was closing his luggage when he heard the elevator ding. "Everyone, go back to your room for your own safety until we figure out what is going on." *Security*, Wilson guessed by the bark in the instructions. He took a seat next to his things and waited. He didn't want to be mistaken for a perpetrator and tased by an overzealous hotel cop.

A thick man popped into the doorway. "Sir, are you all right?"

"Yes, just rattled," Wilson adopted the appropriate guise. "I woke up and saw people in my room. I yelled for help and they took off."

The guard took a look at the sheared metal on the frame and the damage to the door. "How many of them were there?"

"I don't know. It all happened so fast."

"Did you get a good look at any of them?"

"It was dark. All I saw were shadows," Wilson answered

honestly. The guard pulled out a walkie talkie and relayed that the room was secure but the assailants may still be on the premise.

The guard stiffened as Morris rounded the corner, but relaxed once he identified him as a guest; an old man in silk pajamas wasn't a threat. "Sir, please go back to your room. We've got everything under control."

"Like hell you do! What kind of establishment are you people running? What's the world coming to when a man can't rest easy in his own room? Damon, are you all right?" Morris knew the subconscious power of his annoyed black man routine; it was far less likely to get him shot than angry black man would, and it still put people on the defensive.

"It's okay, officer," Wilson addressed the security guard as law enforcement in a deliberate stroke to his ego. "That's my colleague. I called him after I called you." He raised his voice, "I'm in here, Cedric."

"Are you hurt? Did they take anything?" Morris continued his pantomime. He ran his will over Wilson as soon as he made visual contact; there were superficial psychic wounds but nothing critical.

"I'm fine and nothing is missing. I've checked. I just want to forget this ever happened and get some sleep," Wilson replied.

The security guard stepped in. "Sir, we should really call the police and report this."

Wilson wove a little will in his words to help sell the futility of the suggestion. "And tell them what? An unknown number of people that I can't describe broke into my room, took nothing, and didn't physically harm me on the way out?"

He turned to Morris. "I can't stay here tonight. Can I crash in your room, Cedric?"

"Of course," Morris replied and hit the security guard with a little of his mojo. "Surely we can sort this out in the morning. It's too early for this nonsense. My room is 605."

Security acquiesced to what seemed like a reasonable request and the pair walked down the hall to the elevator with Wilson's belongings in tow. "Attempted burglary?" Morris muttered under his breath.

"It was the only thing I could think of on short notice," Wilson whispered.

Chapter Seventeen

Falcon Heights, Minnesota, USA
30th of August, 5:02 a.m. (GMT-5)

Morris arrived early and was the only person at the gate. He flashed a lanyard glamoured to look like a vendor ID and walked into the empty fairgrounds. The grounds weren't open to the public for another hour and the earliest scheduled event was at eight. The only people here this early worked the fair, and even they had enough sense to sleep in on Sunday morning if they could.

The sun was still below the horizon, and only every other light was lit on the dark streets. They saved the juice for when the paying customers were out and about. Morris hadn't intended on coming this early, but he pushed up the timeline after the attack on Wilson. Plus, he was already up and it was always preferable to do these things when the potential for collateral damage was low.

He summoned his will and was pleased the see yesterday's efforts still largely intact. It was like reclaiming land from a swamp: he'd raised parts of the fair's metaphysical landscape during the day and had fully expected the platzgeist to undermine it at night. However, the newly created high ground was barely eroded.

He unconsciously started whistling an old work song as he slowly circumnavigated the grounds but stopped halfway through when he realized he hadn't felt any ghosts this morning. It would be less concerning if it was high noon, but dawn hadn't yet broken. It was still night and even if they were hiding from the platzgeist, there should be traces of them. That's when he realized he also hadn't felt the platzgeist.

"Has it gotten them all?" he worried, picking up the pace. The enchanted items from Orhan's house rattled in his bag as he cut through the center of the grounds. He increased the flow of his will and his tendrils stretched in all directions to their very limit. He was relieved when he finally felt the echoes of ghost activity.

On the periphery, he also sensed the platzgeist and readied for a confrontation. After his burst of will, it knew he was here and he knew where it was. Morris headed east, hot on its trail, but when he turned the corner, it was gone. He beat the bushes, metaphorically speaking, but there was nothing to flush from the cover.

He pumped out more of his will and got a blip on his tendrils, this time north. He zeroed in on its location and took a circuitous route to catch it off guard, but the platzgeist was waiting for him and slipped away before Morris could get his spell off.

It's stronger than yesterday, Morris observed. *And smarter.* After the third time it happened, he got wise to its strategy. It was playing cat and mouse, trying to wear him down without actually giving him battle.

With the ghosts in the items, Morris had no doubt that he could safely take the platzgeist, but only if he could force it to engage. He considered releasing the ghosts and having them help him pin it down, but it was risky. It was nearing dawn, when their power was waning, and he didn't want to give the platzgeist anything else to eat until he had a chance to tweak his strategy.

Rather than tip his hand or waste any more of his energy, he withdrew. The platzgeist was weaker during the day and he needed to regroup. His original plan was to keep Wilson out of this, especially after last night, but that might no longer be possible.

The sun had risen by the time he got back to the hotel, and he knocked twice on the door before pulling out his keycard. After seeing what Wilson had done to the last door when he was surprised, they'd decided to err on the side of caution.

Wilson was still stretched on the couch when he opened the door but was no longer asleep. Morris's knock had woken him, and he rubbed the sleep from his eyes before checking the time. "You're back early. Did you already finish?"

Morris shook his head and started the coffee machine. "No, tricky bastard tried to rope-a-dope me. It would let me get close enough to know it was there and then run away, full speed. I think it's chewed through almost all the ghosts and is using their knowledge of the fair's layout to avoid me. I only had one ping on my radar this morning."

Wilson yawned and stretched. "Probably Haughton. He evaded capture for months in the Philippines after his plane was shot down."

"The good news is that yesterday's efforts are still intact." Morris pulled out his fair map and spread it out on the table for Wilson to review while he sugared and added non-dairy creamer to his coffee.

Fully roused, Wilson padded to the table. It was covered in dots, perfect circles and arcs in red, blue, and black littered across the fair with dates and times on each dot. Had he not known better, he would have assumed a kid had gotten ahold of some geometry tools and had fun with them. "You travel with a compass and protractor?" he asked incredulously.

Morris gave him a sideways look that amounted to "*Don't you?*" and loaded a second cup into the coffee machine. "Each color denotes one of the three groups I've got moving around disturbing the *wa* the platzgeist has with its surroundings. They create a radial effect, and where those radials overlap, there's a synergistic effect."

"The arcs," Wilson surmised.

"Exactly. Those are the locations with the most changes to the metaphysical geography."

Wilson nodded. "Like adding bumpers to a pool table."

"Sort of. Think of it like filling in a wetland. The platzgeist needs water and with enough time and changes, it would get trapped in this pool." Morris indicated the epicenter of all those cascades of arcs. "Unfortunately, we're on day two and the fair is nearly out of ghosts."

Wilson understood the implication. Once the platzgeist ran out of ghosts, it would move onto people, and not just those metaphysically connected to the fair through practicing magic like Orhan and himself. If they didn't pin it down, the state fair was going to have a high body count. He looked at the date and time notations on the circles and worked his way back. "That's a lot of open space, even if you include today's efforts."

"Uh-huh," Morris sounded as he sipped his coffee and brought Wilson the fresh brew. "That's why I couldn't catch the slippery bastard today. He'd got a lot of room to run."

"Can I use your tools?" Wilson asked as he fixed his coffee. "I want to try something out."

Morris unzipped a small black leather shaving bag and withdrew an assortment of geometric tools while Wilson fished out the fair map Jenkin had given him the first day. Wilson weighed down the curling edges with bits of hotel desk kit.

"Before I begin, is there any material difference in effect between your three groups?"

"Not really. They all serve the same function."

"Fair enough," Wilson replied. First, he transcribed what the three groups had done yesterday to his map, making sure the new circles and arcs lined up in the same places as Morris's. He marked those in pen and switched to pencil, making new circles and their subsequent arcs. He may not have Morris's expertise in metaphysical geometry, but he was a master at magical security and a consummate student of military history. Now that he knew the hard limitations—three interchangeable groups, seven stops each, radius of initial effect for each group—he could move the pieces to create a different shape.

When he was done, he stepped back and ran his hands through his short brown hair. "It's a rough sketch, but you get the idea. We don't have to trap it in a pool. We just have to get it to go where we want it to."

It was built on what Morris had started but took a complete different tactic. Instead of the groups going in circles and gradually narrowing the paths, Wilson had them crisscross, like laces on a shoe. The arcs came at odd angles and he smiled when he visualized what Wilson had drawn: a trap with only one way in.

"If you are standing at that opening at the end of the day, it cannot avoid you," Wilson concluded.

Morris looked up and flashed him a grin he'd seen often but never been on the receiving end of. It was the equivalent of a bear hug without contact. "I like it, but this is a bad location. It's too close to the main entrance. We want a low density area."

Wilson took the same shape and moved it around in his head. "How about near all the stock barns? All the events are usually over by five," Wilson spit balled.

"Not a good idea. Lots of animals there; we could have a mini-stamped if it spooks them good," Morris pointed out.

Wilson looked for another spot within yesterday's arcs. "Somewhere in North End?"

Morris shook his head. "I was just there this morning. There's a 5k walk against Cancer this evening taking place over the entire North-Northeastern section of the fair."

"That's leaves us with slim pickings, Morris." Wilson sighed. "Only the midway's left if we use what you did yesterday, and that's always going to be packed at night."

"Maybe not." Morris grunted and pulled out his phone. He hit the fair's website and scrolled for more information. "There's a big concert at the grandstand, a rock 'n' roll band. Between that, the Cancer walk, and the play in the amphitheater, we should see less traffic in the midway."

"It'll still be open," Wilson objected.

"*Everything* is going to be open *all* the time," Morris countered. "If we wait until the fair is closed, that would be after midnight. I can't avoid having to confront it on its home turf, but there's no need to do it when it's even stronger at night, not to mention all the people it could kill in the meantime if we're misjudging our timing. Which we could be."

Wilson conceded the point as he erased the pencil marks

and started replotting his trap to end at the midway. He left the dots unlabeled, leaving the actual assignment of groups to Morris. "How's that look?"

"Good, but there are so many gaps between each performance to the next. The trap only works if it stays within the laces," Morris pointed out as he played it out in his mind from the platzgeist's perspective. "What's to stop him from going north here instead of south?"

"You," Wilson said simply. "It's afraid of you. When we want it to go south, you stand to the north." He plucked an example out of military history to further illustrate his point. "The platzgeist is trying to Fabien Strategy you. The strategy comes from the Roman general Fabius Maximus during the Second Punic War where he used it against Hannibal. It's basically one of avoidance of a pitched battle in favor of smaller skirmishes designed to wear you down over time. It doesn't want to meet you head on. Wherever you are is where it's *not* going to be."

Morris skipped over the history lesson and focused on one word. "We?"

"I assume I'll be there. How else are you going to use me as bait?" Wilson asked.

Morris was glad that Wilson had reached the same conclusion as he had because it wasn't the sort of thing he liked to order someone else to do. "If you're volunteering, I do have a few ideas of how to draw the platzgeist to you. But first, I've got to reassign my people. Their first performance is at nine, and I need to give them as much notice as possible if I'm going to change their itinerary," he replied, grabbing the colored pens and assigning each dot a group and time.

Chapter Eighteen

Falcon Heights, Minnesota, USA
30th of August, 7:27 p.m. (GMT-5)

The midway was the heart of every fair, from the humble county gathering with its strong agricultural emphasis to the wider cultural focus of the state fair. For the price of admission, everyone could walk the midway and soak in the bright lights, happy music, and communal spirit of the modern day promenade.

Regardless of its location, the midway offered two unique features—rides and games—both of which were designed to rake in the dough. The universal midway currency for carnival rides was tickets that visitors had to buy in fixed bundled amounts upfront. People inevitably exited the gates with extra tickets in their pockets. Either because they didn't have enough to do the thing they wanted to do without having to buy more, or because they over-bought to avoid having to stand in line for more. It didn't amount to much per person, but when multiplied over total attendance, all those paid for but unused tickets were pure profit for the fair.

Then there were the games of skill. Everyone knew they

were rigged, but the call of the barkers and the shiny prizes always drew people in. The desire to play in spite of the odds was embedded deep in the human psyche because a win was totemic of a larger victory: a David versus Goliath tableau with more bells and whistles.

The window dressing changed over time, but the basic games were always there—knock over the milk bottles, pop the balloons with a dart, aim the water cannon into the target—simple motor skills everyone could do. The appearance of ease was an integral part of the lure. The inspectors tried to keep the games honest, but only the person setting up the milk bottles knew if the bottom ones were weighted.

In some ways, it was like going to a magic show—the audience *wanted* to believe in the spectacle. That was part of the entertainment factor. But there was always someone who found more joy in pointing out how the tricks worked. Wilson was all too willing to be that guy.

He'd arrived at the fair an hour ago to take stock of his options and blew twenty dollars on games to find his targets. Thirty minutes ago, Morris had sent him a text letting him know everything was going according to plan. He bided his time with fried cheese curds, fried pickles, and the best draft root beer he'd ever had.

Once the slim minute hand of his Girard-Perregaux ticked down to 7:30, Wilson focused his will and directed it at his first target: the ring toss. *Think, think, think…* The arrow of his will hit the thin yellow plastic ring that was barely wider than the bottleneck in midair. Instead of bouncing off, it landed true.

"What a toss!" the attendant called out. Knowing that it was a fluke, he used it to draw in more potential players. "We have a contender. Two more wins and you can pick something from the top row."

The top row was loaded with the good stuff: giant oversized stuffed animals and battery-operated toys. The middle row—which took two wins—was less impressive but still more appealing than the bottom row, which was packed with dinky little plushies that would decorate baby strollers, desks, dashboards, and the back window of cars before landing in a donation box.

Wilson sipped his root beer as he tapped his will twice more and the little girl picked a teddy bear almost as big as her. He moved on to the next player throwing blue rings, then a third tossing red, and by the time the white rings rimmed the bottles, the barker was befuddled and the growing crowd was excited.

He kept at it and over the next fifteen minutes, every single throw was a winner. The children laughed and giggled and people gathered to watch what the news would later report as the "Miracle on the Midway." It had all the frenetic energy of a hot slot machine in a casino with the childlike wonder of a carnival. A visible wave of relief washed over the haggard barker's face when Wilson relented and the game returned to its normal odds, but the magic of the moment lingered even as the crowd dispersed.

He then moved deeper into the midway, coming closer to the dead end the sextet had created earlier this morning. His next game of skill was the free throw. The smaller-than-regulation hoop was slightly oblong, making it less forgiving if the overinflated ball hit the rim. For the next fifteen minutes, every ball was nothing but net and the crowds gathered quicker this time. Ring toss was a kiddie game, but free throw? Everyone knew that took skill.

Promptly at eight, Wilson hit his third mark at the very end of the midway: the dart toss. The colorful underinflated balloons fluttered on the board in the light breeze, impervious to the dull points of the light darts. For the quarter hour, the rapid staccato of balloons bursting sounded like popcorn popping.

Tasks completed, he did his best impression of Deacon, sending out his stubby tendrils to "get a feel" for the place. He couldn't get more than ten feet out, but he could tell his efforts were paying off. Wilson had laid out a trail of breadcrumbs for the hungry and harried platzgeist. The midway was metaphysically lit up with a flashing neon "Diner" sign.

Now, all he had to do was wait. He found a place between the booths he'd lit up near the entrance to the midway and positioned himself in the median between the two directions of pedestrian traffic. The only way he could have advertised harder as bait was to dress in a meat suit.

He readied his will as the sun began to set. He had a rough idea of what to expect based on his previous run-ins with the platzgeist. It used his memories, raking up old fears, and the conflict didn't occur in the physical realm. It was a battle of wills, not fists or guns, and it was going to be more difficult at the fair—the platzgeist was weaker the further away it moved from its generative real estate. But Wilson didn't have to win: he just had to hold out until Deacon arrived.

The crowd thinned as more visitors left for other engagements and fewer people entered the midway. Wilson started to worry that something had gone wrong as it grew darker. Did the last performance not work? Had the platzgeist squeezed through a narrow gap? Perfect circles and arcs may have worked on paper, but that didn't mean they always mapped to real life.

Then, a sudden flare of goosebumps washed over him right when the sun finally kissed the horizon goodbye. *It was just timing its arrival to its advantage*, Wilson realized just before the full force of the platzgeist bore down upon him. The world turned gray and movement slowed. Even though his body was still standing in the midway, his mind was somewhere else.

Sound seemed distant and hollow as everything changed in front of him. He was no longer in Minnesota, but walking the midway of the Northern Idaho State Fair, hand-in-hand with his father. Despite the fact that he was a grown man, his hand was engulfed by his father's calloused one.

This particular memory wasn't bad in and of itself. In fact, it had been one of the few moments of joy he'd known with the man, but as Wilson aged, the memory had become increasingly bitter. It became an indictment, proof of what had been possible. It demonstrated everything that he'd lost before he was even conscious enough to understand what that had really meant. His father knew how to be kind and protective, which meant every time he wasn't, it was a *choice*.

Wilson focused his will on his hand, slamming the tactile memory out of his flesh until he could no longer feel the roughened skin. As he did so, the crowd moving around him became translucent before disappearing entirely. The bright lights behind him shut down in sequence and a wave of darkness crashed over him before passing to the rest of the fair. But the inky abyss didn't stop there. It rolled through the entire city, unrelenting, until everything was black.

It's not real, Wilson reminded himself, will behind his words, but the darkness grew deeper and fuller and colder. There was a dim glow around him that reminded him of the twinkling lights he'd seen in the trailer, except he wasn't looking at the shadow. He was in it.

The lights flickered and he heard clicking. It spent shivers down his spine as he registered its origin: talons of karakura demons. The last time he'd heard that sound, he was in the mines of Utashinai, Japan. He fought to control his racing heart and gasped in pain as his side flared at the memory of their claws tearing through him even though he no longer bore their scars. The light extinguished and he was once again in complete blackness, terrified. He fired his Glock repeatedly, making his best guess on where one of the creatures would be from the previous flash of the muzzle.

It's not real, Wilson repeated, forging his will into an electric sword. He slashed the blade through the darkness, revealing the Minnesota midway behind the paper-thin facade the platzgeist had created. He looked for Deacon, but he never stopped swinging.

With each swipe, he cut away more of the mines but to his horror, the razor-sharp edge sliced through the fair. It was no more real than a matte painting in a movie, a mere backdrop to disguise reality. Light pierced the midway at night with each cut, revealing the deeper existence that had always been lying underneath. The dark thing he'd always known but had refused to acknowledge.

The sword disappeared from his hands and he found himself standing in waves of golden ripe grain, roiling in a soft breeze. Rolling green hills stretched in all directions as far as the eye could see, and he could smell the apple trees he knew lay between the hills, just out of sight. Above him, the sheep-like clouds dotted the endless cerulean sky.

I haven't made it out, he realized in a moment of terrifying clarity. *I'm still in Avalon. I failed.* He trembled with exhaustion and starvation. *If I don't harvest something soon, I'll have another hungry night, and I can't afford that.*

He looked down at himself and saw that his clothes were in tatters, the tunics, belt, and shoes he'd taken from the entombed dead. In his ragged hands, his black-bladed utility knife had been worn down to such an extent that it looked like a filleting blade. He clumsily rushed to fill his hands with whatever grain he could carry because night, and winter, was rushing toward him. Hands full of stalks, he trudged the worn path to the small windowless rock hut that he'd built when he'd arrived, when he was flush with muscle and fat, not at all like the walking skeleton he was now.

He cried out loud when he saw there wasn't a trickle of smoke coming out of the doorway. His fire had gone out. *Stupid! Stupid! Stupid! How are you going to make it through the winter night without heat?* When he got inside, he wearily dropped the grain next to his grinding stone and picked up the remains of his firestarter set. The metal scraper had an indention from repeated contact with the magnesium strike rod. As he fit the pair together and quickly moved them to create the sparks he so desperately needed, the rod broke into several small pieces.

Cursing, he tried to find one long enough to generate a spark, but they were all too short. Outside the sun had set and the cold was rolling in fast. Fireless, foodless, he huddled in the corner where he'd made a rats' nest of a bed out of all the wheat stalks he'd harvested. Desperately he burrowed into the pile. He swept his emaciated arms around him, covering up as best he could, but the cold was harsh and quick and he could already see his breath pluming in the bitterly cold hut.

There were gasps as Wilson collapsed in the middle of the walkway, and people rushed to him. In the commotion, they paid no mind to Morris as he stepped into the midway. Atop of Wilson, like a lover, the platzgeist fed, oblivious to his approach.

Morris brushed his hand in a small gesture, like shooing a fly, and the shadow was knocked off Wilson, buffeted by the force of the older man's will. It turned its ebon head and fear rippled through its being at the sight of Morris's luminescence. Panicked, it struck back with all its might. For a brief moment, the air surrounding Morris swelled with the scents of Mississippi at the height of summer, coupled with motor oil, new leather, and brimstone.

Fool, old men don't fear the past; they fear the future, he said to the creature as he brought his will against it. Although his words were not spoken, they rumbled with gravitas and pinned the shadowy form to the ground. He walked to where it lay, sidestepping the gawkers that were circling Wilson's prone body, and dropped a brown paper lunch bag containing all the items Orhan had manufactured onto its chest.

He then brought his heel down with a shadowy explosion, breaking the metaphysical chains that bound the ghosts within. Freed from their restraints and furiously angry, they pounced upon the platzgeist. Their human features twisted and shifted into their terrifying forms as they tore at it like a pack of dogs upon a fox.

As they worked their pointed teeth into the blackness, Morris molded his will into a spear and planted it into the shadow's side. Then he raised his other arm to the sky. Even though it was evening, he found the sun's radiance and his unuttered will echoed out into the great expanse as a bolt of lightning crashed down upon him. The searing brilliance shot through the spear and into the shadow. There was an unearthly howl, and then the platzgeist was no more. In its place stood all the ghosts it had absorbed. Satisfied that justice had been served, the ghosts took their human forms and greeted their lost comrades.

Morris left the spirits to their reunion and turned his attention to the mortal realm. "I'm a doctor!" he called out as he pushed his way through the circle that had formed around Wilson. He put his hands on the smaller man's throat, pretending to check for a pulse. It was ice cold. "It's okay. He's got a pulse," he declared before anyone tried heroic measures such as CPR or AEDs—they weren't going to save him. He gathered his will and pumped the warmth of summer into Wilson's body.

In his mind's Avalon, the freezing Wilson heard a sudden crackle of burning logs. Even as the heat pushed back the cold, he didn't trust his senses. He pushed his head out of the straw pile and almost wept when he saw the full flame in the hovel's crude hearth. Within the roaring fire was a small figure with six wings: two covering its face, two covering its feet, and two that held it aloft. Although the winged creature didn't resemble Morris, it spoke in his voice. "Time to come back to reality."

Wilson closed his eyes and everything melted away. When he opened his eyes again, he saw Morris's face, brow furrowed in concern. "Is it done?" he asked softly.

Morris smiled. "All done. How do you feel?"

"As cold as Dante's Hell, but I ain't dead yet." He tried moving his extremities and found them stiff from the lingering chill. "Help me up before someone calls the paramedics."

"He's all right!" Morris called out theatrically as he gave Wilson a hand standing up. "I'm going to walk him to the first aid station. Thanks for your help, everyone." He put just enough will in his words to nudge everyone back to whatever they were doing. It was being handled by a professional now; they weren't needed.

The movement circulated the warmth around his body and within minutes, Wilson stopped shivering. "Are the ghosts okay?"

"In fit and fighting form, which is more than I can say about you," Morris voiced his worry. "Is there anything I can get you?"

"A hot shower, a warm bed, and a week of sleep would be great," Wilson replied. "But I'll settle for one of those warm chocolate chip cookies you mentioned."

Epilogue

Detroit, Michigan, USA
9th of September, 4:15 p.m. (GMT-4)

Wilson adjusted his crimson tie in the visor mirror of his 911. He'd gone with a tight cape knot and he wanted it to be perfectly symmetrical. He only had one chance to make a first impression. When he was satisfied, he grabbed his attaché, exited and secured his car, and headed east toward the casino.

His destination was only a few blocks away from his downtown gym and he availed himself to their parking garage over street parking or the casino's lot. Plus, the walk let him get some of his nervous energy out before arriving.

He kept to the shade as much as possible until he reached the steakhouse. It smelled amazing, but he didn't enter through the heavy glass double doors for a late lunch. Instead, he climbed the two flights of stairs to the third floor.

There weren't any signs advertising that he'd entered the office of Dr. Sylvia Kamiński, but the decor was undeniably outpatient medical services, down to the rows of vinyl seats in the waiting area, the array of old magazines, and a receptionist on the phone sitting behind a sliding glass window.

She motioned for Wilson to take a seat and he had the pick of the place. There was no one else in the waiting area, and he opted for a seat by the bank of windows along the north wall. From there, he had a good view of the receptionist, the front door, the interior door leading into the heart of the practice, and the casino parking garages across the street.

Think, think, think… He summoned his will and ran it over the room, checking for wards. There was nothing to be found, which gave him pause. He didn't have much experience with therapists beyond passing CIA psych evals, and the fact that this psychiatrist practiced above a steakhouse didn't bolster his confidence in the process. She was supposed to be someone he could talk to about all things, but he found the lack of security concerning. Had not Leader herself recommended Dr. Kamiński and told him she'd had been vetted at the highest levels, he would have canceled the appointed and walked out, but he stayed in his seat.

He watched the receptionist hang up and type on her computer in his periphery before he heard the heavy glass slide open. "Thanks for your patience. How can I help you this afternoon?" she greeted him.

Wilson stood and walked up to the window. He was a private person and wasn't about to yell his business across the room, even if it was empty. "I have a 4:30 appointment with Dr. Kamiński."

"To ensure patient confidentiality, would you mind telling me your full name?" she asked politely instead of providing the name she had on the schedule.

Wilson approved even though he wasn't fond of anyone asking personal questions. "David Wilson," he replied evenly.

She smiled and handed him a stack of paperwork clipped to a board with a pen. "Thank you, Mr. Wilson. There are a few things I need you to fill out and sign. The first is a questionnaire about your medical history. The second is consent for treatment and billing. The third is a copy of our HIPAA policy. That's for you, but if you sign the final page to attest that we have provided that to you, we'll keep that for our records. When you're done with that, bring it back to me along with your photo ID and proof of insurance."

She dismissed Wilson with a smile and slid the glass pane as he walked back to his seat. It felt weird filling in his actual private information. He felt exposed in a way he didn't when he used his given name as part of his FBI, CIA, or Interpol covers. He extracted his driver's license from his wallet and returned to the front five minutes later.

"I'll be self-pay," he informed her when he failed to produce an insurance card. Removing a third party payer meant one less entity informed of his visit.

The receptionist nodded and did a quick sweep to make sure all the essential areas were completed before matching the picture on the card to the man standing in front of her. She passed his ID into a scanner and checked the files on her screen before handing it back to him. "Everything looks in order. The doctor will be with you shortly." He nodded and waited until he was back in his seat before putting it back in his leather wallet.

A few minutes later, he heard the indistinct sound of a conversation on the other side of the glass. He picked out three different female voices, but the chipper receptionist was the only one he could understand with any certainty. The interior door opened, and a woman wearing sunglasses and a wide-brimmed hat walked through the lobby on her way to the exit. The sharp clacks of her heels resonated on the wooden floor and he could hear the echo of her steps on the stairs. He watched her sashay across the street to the parking garages and found himself wondering if she was a special client, like himself.

The interior door opened again and the receptionist was on the other side. "Mr. Wilson, Dr. Kamiński will see you now," she informed him. He rose and followed her down a short corridor. The first thing he noticed was the impressive array of wards that led to the threshold of the door at the end of the hall, and his esteem for the good doctor rose considerably. He found himself wanting to spend more time examining them but he kept pace when the receptionist cleared her throat.

When she opened the door, she introduced him to the well-dressed woman standing in the center of the room. "Dr. Kamiński, this is David Wilson, your 4:30."

The room was a world apart from the waiting area. Crossing the threshold was like stepping back in time. There was nothing modern or clinical about it. The walls were lined with built-in dark-stained walnut bookshelves filled with tanned leather books. Even the bare walls were covered with board and batten paneling, stained to perfectly blend into the shelves.

In one corner, there was a red leather chaise longue with a purple and gold afghan draped over its classical lines for those that wanted to recline for the full Freudian experience. In the opposite corner was a large wooden desk, but there wasn't a computer, laptop, or phone in sight. In between stood a long table with a bowl of fruit, a pitcher of water and four glasses, and an open antique traveling medicine cabinet resplendent with tiny labeled bottles and vials.

"Thank you, Sally," the doctor replied and introduced herself with an extended hand. "Mr. Wilson, I'm Sylvia Kamiński. Please, take a seat." She motioned to one of the three walnut Chippendale armchairs while she took their singular hazelnut brown companion. Wilson's will felt the wards snap into place as soon as the receptionist closed the door behind her.

He immediately started analyzing the woman as he shook her hand: average height and build, early forties, brown hair and eyes, and a stark, angular face like a hunting bird's. Her jewelry was expensive without being gauche, and there was nothing personal on or around her desk: no pictures, diplomas, cards, or whimsical items. He took a seat, placing his attaché next to the chair where he could see it in his peripheral vision.

"I understand this is your first visit?"

Wilson was taken aback by the question. "Yes, that is correct."

The fine lines around her mouth and eyes deepened as she smiled. "Then allow me to explain the setup. I offer a full range of psychiatric services for people who must have full confidence in my ability to provide absolute confidentiality. I achieve that through wards and the cabinet of Dr. Caligari." She placed her hand on the open mahogany box.

"As in the movie?" Wilson asked skeptically.

"Same name, very different cabinet," she reassured him. "This one was made in the 1820s and has an uncertain history until the 1890s when it was used by the Butcher of Flensburg in the commissioning of his horrible crimes. Fortunately, I've been able to find more constructive uses for it."

She removed one of the vials. "This is pure burdock powder, harmless in and of itself, but when coupled with the power of the cabinet, it can be used to erase the memory of the user for the next hour." She opened the top, snorted from the vial, and recapped it. Then she returned the vial to its nook, closed the cabinet and opened it again. She withdrew a small hourglass and flipped it, placing it on the table. "This means I won't remember what we talk about as long as I close the cabinet before our time is up. My memory of our visit will remain in the cabinet. The next time you come, I'll inhale the powdered burdock and the memory of all our previous discussions will return. I'll do this every time you visit.

"The magic of the burdock only works when you are present— that's what triggers which memories return. It won't work if someone or something dons your likeness because they aren't you. It only works with my free will. I cannot be charmed into using it nor can I be forced under duress. It is the highest level of privacy that can be acquired. Keep your eyes on the sand in the hourglass, Mr. Wilson, and know that at long as it still falls, no one will learn any of your secrets from me." She paused, hands folded in her lap, and waited. They always had questions.

"What about your notes?" Wilson inquired.

"I don't take any. One of the benefits of the cabinet is that the memories of our discussions are always fresh in my mind. There's no need to take notes because nothing is forgotten. Sally informs me you are a cash patient, which removes the necessity of making false progress notes of your visit for insurance reimbursement, which is a service I provide for my clients that use insurance."

"What about mundane surveillance equipment?" he probed.

"My office is swept quarterly by a private security firm and the windows are triple-paned to prevent parabolic microphones," she replied. Her answer was direct and firm and her tone even and calm, all of which Wilson found comforting but he wasn't one to rest of another's word.

He nodded. "Fair enough, but if you don't mind, I'd like to perform my own security assessment."

She opened her hands. "It's your hour, Mr. Wilson."

He retrieved his attaché and released the clasps on the case as soon as Dr. Kamiński agreed. He retrieved one of Weber's devices—a bug sniffer that functioned as a radio frequency detector, a non-linear junction detector, and a magnetic frequency detector. "It shouldn't take long."

He walked around the room, ensuring that there weren't any electronic listening devices. When he'd covered the entire room, he retrieved four black bricklike pieces of electronica. He placed one unit in each corner of the room and then hit a trigger on the sniffer. The room was suffused by a loud white noise that Wilson dialed back using a special control on Weber's device. "   These will interfere with all active listening devices and offer particular protection against laser microphones," he explained, sitting back down and pointing at the small stained-glass window over the table.

"As you like," Dr. Kamiński said neutrally. If she took offense, she didn't show it. She waited for him to settle into his seat before starting the session in earnest. "First, I'd like to welcome you and give us an opportunity to get to know each other better. Think of this as an introductory session to see if future ones would be fruitful. Mutual trust is the foundation of therapy and that only comes with time and understanding.

With that in mind, why don't you tell me what brings you to my practice?"

The question was so wide open, and Wilson had a brief moment of analysis paralysis. His first instinct was always to obfuscate, but to tell her an outright lie would defeat the purpose of coming altogether. Instead, he answered with a small truth.

"My cat won't stop bothering me about it." He watched Kamiński's face to see if his words had any impact, but found no trace of judgment or disbelief.

"And how does your cat do that?" she responded without missing a beat.

"A mutual acquaintance gave me your card and when I didn't make an appointment, she started leaving your card on my coffee machine." It was true, even if not the whole truth.

Dr. Kamiński smiled. "I've had patients referred in lots of unique ways, but never 'by cat' before. I'm assuming she's magical of some sort. A familiar?"

"Something like that," he said vaguely.

She picked up on his resistance and went a different direction. "It sounds like you've had my card for some time. Besides your cat's persistence, what convinced you to make an appointment?"

Wilson paused before answering, carefully choosing his words. "Things have changed recently and I'm finding it difficult to focus the way I used to be able to. I thought I was coping with it all right, but it's starting to affect my work and I really can't afford to be anything but one hundred percent. If I make a mistake on the job, people could die."

Dr. Kamiński nodded to show that she was actively listening. "It sounds like your work is very important to you. Would you like to tell me what you do for a living?"

Wilson took a deep breath before answering. "I'm a field agent for the Salt Mine."

She tilted her head to one side. "That must be stressful for you. Any job that requires high amounts of secrecy can be isolating and make it difficult to form connections and maintain healthy relationships. But when someone works in the Salt Mine, there are extremely few people that really understand the kinds of things agents battle on a day-to-day basis to monitor and neutralize dangerous magic and supernatural phenomena." Her simple but insightful statement dumbfounded Wilson.

"You aren't the first from your organization that has had need of my services, although I can honestly say I can't recall them." She smiled at her own joke. "You mentioned changes. What's changed?"

Wilson appreciated the artistry in her modulation. They'd just met yet her question sounded sincerely interested, like it came from an old friend.

"It all started last year, when I got my soul back," he replied.

"What do you mean by that?" she asked. It was a petition for more information, but at his own pace and from his perspective.

Wilson watched the grains of sand fall in the hourglass as he decided to take the plunge. "About six years ago, I almost died but my partner brought me back. I ended up with a little of his soul, and for about five years, I was only partly myself. To fix that, I made a bargain with Baba Yaga to rend away the parts that weren't mine so the rest of me could heal properly. She did it, but something went awry and I was shunted into Avalon very much alive. I had to burn part of my life force to try to escape and I might have died again in the process. It's unclear. But before I maybe-died, I managed to bargain my way out and gained my cat in the process. She acquired sentience when she accidentally ate part of my soul rescuing me."

Dr. Kamiński said nothing, letting the words fall into the white noise.

"Huh," Wilson snorted. "When I say it all out loud and in a row, it makes sense why I'm having some difficulties adjusting."

"Is it okay if I call you David?" Dr. Kamiński asked.

Of all the questions she could have asked, that was the last one on his list, but it struck him as respectful of his disclosure. "Sure."

*****

Wilson closed the door behind him and walked down the stairs. He felt less distant from himself than he had in a long time. Given his situation, he'd never considered therapy as a realistic option for him. Ever since Alex had been supposedly killed by a wendigo, he hadn't had anyone that he could talk to and he never really spoke with his coworkers. Indecision or uncertainty wasn't what someone who was relying upon you to cover their back wanted to hear. And if he was being honest, he didn't really want to share with them anyway. They were just the people he worked with. Alex had been different. Spending time with him had been effortless, and he wished things had gone differently.

He was so lost in thought on the walk back to his car that he almost missed the small black shape sitting in the passenger's seat of his 911. He lowered his will when he saw the flickering tail and bright green eyes. "What are you doing here?" he asked Mau after he opened the door.

I wanted to judge the power of your swnw, she responded.

"Swnw? What's a Swnw?"

The healer. Why do I take the time to tell you the real name of things if you don't remember?

"Sorry, I'd forgotten. I was pretty sleepy at the time," Wilson excused himself. "I think things went well."

The cat saw Crawling Shadow was still agitated and gave her own opinion on the matter. *He didn't do a very good job. You are still unsettled.*

"She," he corrected. "And one visit isn't going to magically fix everything. It doesn't work that way, Mau."

Then it would be better to fix yourself. Have you tried licking it?

Wilson turned in his seat to face the cat. "It's not that kind of wound, but that's basically what therapy is—a person learning how to fix themselves or learning how to reach a state where they're satisfied with where they are. This swnw is supposed to help someone learn how to be the way they want to be."

Mau was pleased he used the correct word, even if his pronunciation was questionable and his answer unsatisfactory. *So how long will this take?*

"I don't know. Today was just to meet each other and get a mutual understanding of goals and concerns. I think she's someone I can work with, but it could take a while," Wilson answered honestly without giving hard numbers.

Mau sighed. *Are you such a slow learner?*

"No faster than anyone else, I'm afraid," Wilson chuckled wryly. "I may be able to do a lot of extraordinary things, Mau, but at the end of the day I'm still just a human."

The silence stretched as the cat said nothing in reply, and eventually Wilson asked, "You going to jump home?"

No, I want to ride in your vehicle with the wind in my face. She pressed the window button to crack the window but nothing happened as Wilson hadn't started the car. *Make it work*, she ordered, pressing it repeatedly with increasing annoyance, *and drive me home.*

"It's rush hour, Mau," Wilson warned as the Porsche

hummed to life. "We're not going to be able to go very fast."

Mau pressed her paw on the button and sat taller when the glass obeyed her. *I will make do.*

THE END

The agents of The Salt Mine will return in *Double Dutch*

Printed in Great Britain
by Amazon

81156141R00112